Andrew Brice

The Mobiad

Battle of the voice - An heroic-comic poem, sportively satirical

Andrew Brice

The Mobiad
Battle of the voice - An heroic-comic poem, sportively satirical

ISBN/EAN: 9783337196325

Printed in Europe, USA, Canada, Australia, Japan

Cover: Foto ©Andreas Hilbeck / pixelio.de

More available books at **www.hansebooks.com**

THE
MOBIAD:

OR,

BATTLE of the VOICE.

AN

HEROI-COMIC POEM,

SPORTIVELY SATIRICAL:

Being a briefly hiftorical, natural and lively, free and humorous, DESCRIPTION

OF AN

EXETER ELECTION.

In SIX CANTO'S.

Illuftrated with fuch NOTES as for *fome* Readers may be fuppofed ufeful.

By DEMOCRITUS JUVENAL, Moral Profeffor of Ridicule, and plaguy-pleafant Fellow of Stingtickle College;

Vulgarly

ANDREW BRICE, EXON.

- - - - Magno in populo cum fæpe coorta eft
Seditio, fævitque animis ignobile vulgus,
Infequitur clamorque virûm, furor arma miniftrat,
Præfentemque viris intentant omnia mortem;
Difficile eft fatiram non fcribere.— Ridiculum acri
Fortiùs et meliùs magnas plerumque fecat res.

VIRG. JUV. HOR.

EXON: Printed and Sold by BRICE and THORN: And fold alfo by T. DAVIES, in Great-Ruffel Street, Covent-Garden, London. MDCCLXX.

The Author's Valedictory Sermon to this hopeful Spark, his Progeny.

GO, thou playfome, flily-fnickering, dry-bobbing Son of PHANTASY. That frolic Dame was *honeftly* thy Mother ; conceiv'd, form'd, and with no hard Travail — (*Indignation* aiding) — brought thee forth. HISTORIC TRUTH, however, had a finger in the pye, and (as another trite Saying goes) blow'd to thy making. Go ; — try thy Fortune, as thy Betters have done. As Circumftances allow'd, I brought thee up to ---- what thou art ; have now tolerably cloath'd thee in a decent plain Suit of Print : And what is to be done next but fend thee into the World ? Good Hands receive thee, and not harfhly treat thee ! And may'ft thou beft thrive in thy proper Vocation of *pleafing* and *profiting* thy Entertainers !

I fhould gladly have had beftow'd upon thee a fhort Teftimonial of fome or other Worthinefs, or good Property, in thee ; or elfe to have got fome Refpectab e Name for thy Protection. But Patronage for Poetry, 'fhou'd feem, is now no more the *Growth of every Clime* than is good Poetry itfelf. And alas ! VIRGILS thrive not but in the cultivated warm Garden of a MOECENAS. Kind Fofterers, — (One Swallow making of itfelf - - - but One) — and even a tutelary Mafter, feem as difficultly to be met with. So that, at the laft refort, thou muft for *a good Run* truft to thy own Legs ; — or, as fome Folk feem to think, to the compulfive Conduct of thy own PLANET : A Guide very precarious truly ; there being, they tell you, amongft the others, a villainous *Twelve-farthing* one, a cruel Envier of Merit, malicioufly more bufy with his Influence than all the reft. If fuch their Creed be orthodox, that mifchievous Meddler, perhap, too much tamper'd with my own Nativity: Forcing upon me a radical Itch of Scribbling, nay an ungainful *poetic Turn* ; when SATURN himfelf might have taken me under

Why, then, might not fuch, in a fort, behold
himfelf, as it were in a Mirrour, in Hogarth's
Midnight Conversation, or fome antick
Chimney-piece more vulgarly baccanalian? Why
fhould the Moral of the pencil'd Satire be over-
look'd or difregarded? One might be apt to fancy
Tavern - Quarrels, painted artfully in Tipling-
Rooms, might, if confiderately obferv'd, withold
real Gentlemen of Breeding from plunging into
fuch Depths of Liquor as might overwhelm their
Humanity, and transform them for a Time to
fuch worfe than Savages as in Colours reprefented.
And we fhould imagine, a Man, in calm good
Temper, might hate, yet defpife, his own late
Appearance pourtray'd the very Madman he
look'd, and behav'd, in Height of that Rage he
was, ftrangely he might think, thrown into.

And wherefore fhould not the Effect hold in
parallel Examples? Why might not fome heed-
fully perufing a boifterous Election, in which
they were Agents or Agitators, (efpecially of but
little if any Moment) juftly defcrib'd in *fuited
Verfe,* be afham'd of the ridiculous or bafe Parts
which they, as 'twere in Effigie, review they acted
in the wretched Farce? Why fhould they not feel
a Twinge of Thought at the Dangers which they,
with others, prov'd inftrumental — (though, it
may be, unwittingly) — in occafioning, as well as
Remorfe at being any Way, even undefignedly,
acceffary to, Mifchiefs therein committed?

This

This Poetic Sketch was drawn to that honeſt Intent. Though there are very few, if any, directly and perſonally charactteriz'd, yet Numbers, if they have Eyes of Underſtanding, may diſcern their own Images in Deſcription expoſing themſelves to Deriſion, Contempt, perhaps and Deteſtation. Alſo may be ſeen to what a diſtracted and unhappy Plight mere Whim and Fantaſt have brought us. Why then ſhould it not conduce to the correcting our Conduct, diſcountenancing Tumult, reſtoring Civility at leaſt, and by Degrees recovering Trade, ſo fooliſhly deſtroy'd by harebrain'd Faction? Why may we not hope thereupon that Perſons of Equanimity may venture into publick and mix'd Converſation, be there us'd with Good-manners, and ſee the Company ſit, and in due Seaſon part, obſequious and mannerly at worſt, — notwithſtanding their having voted differently for a *Forty Man* (as they ſtyle him), a Mayor, or Member of Parliament himſelf?

Though dreading a being ſurrounded in and by a M O B, eſpecially a pent-up contending one, yet, to make proper Obſervations, and to collect apt Materials, I, for once, voluntarily hazarded myſelf even on the very Spot of thickeſt Uproar and Confuſion. At which Time, worſe than that of the Painter (who, ſurpaſſingly to delineate a Battle, in its various Horrors, to the Life, went joyfully to gaze at one, but therein loſt both his Arms by his Curioſity) had like to have prov'd my Hap; not only almoſt cruſh'd to death in the

a 2 Throng,

Throng, but like to have my fmall Portion of Brains prefs'd out, or my Head itfelf wrung off, in the Gateway, endeavouring, at laft, to efcape out of the crowded Hall.

However rough, unfinifhed, and incorrect, yea trifling and filly, the flight Performance be, or fhall be faid to be, — my Vanity flatters itfelf it is pretty natural, picturefque, and indifferently full of genuine Humour: Which are Hits and Ingredients not defpicable in Pieces of this Nature. Yes, I am forward enough to fancy, that it is not quite devoid of fuch titillating as well as poignant *Humour* as may divert even where it nettles, pleafe the Struck in defpight of their Refentment, and force them at leaft to fmile juft upon biting their Lips or Knuckles.

It being calculated principally for the Ufe and Service of *this City*, — (though not to be *fo very local* as not to fit other Places; — M o b s being M o b s every-where) — as well as the Subject is a Tranfaction upon the Spot, I thought fit to gather many of the collateral Incidents, Similes, Allufions, and other embellifhing Circumftances, as well as fome Words and Phrafes of Propriety, from the proper Scene of Action, and Parts adjacent ; fo as to adapt the Poem moft properly to the *Place.* The *Time* of the Main Action alfo confifts of about *Six Hours* ; each diftinguifh'd properly by concomitant Tokens, well known to the
Inhabitants.

Inhabitants. In managing of which, though the
more ftreighten'd thereby of Fancy, I have had
this one Advantage of fervile mechanic Imitators,
and Common ‑ place Authors, *viz.* of writing
Things certainly *my own*, yea alfo, fuch as they
are! probably *new*.

But, as it's not impoffible it may likewife fall
into the Hands of Strangers, and at a Diftance,
and live too when the prefent Generation have all
left the Light, I have in the Bottom Margin furnifh'd fuch with explanatory Notes, as well as illi-
terate Readers among ourfelves with a few others,
which they may need, feverally, to apprehend
Matters by.

Now, if the neighbourly prime E N D of it be
happily attain'd, let the Execution itfelf be laugh'd
at, defpis'd, or vilify'd, as much as thofe who knów
any or no Reafon for it pleafe. Real Errors, as
well as fmaller Slips, *quæ aut incuria fudit, &c.* —
(As where is the Work which has of all been
thought abfolutely clear of 'em ; — fince even that
of P O P E himfelf has not appear'd infallible ;) —
are, I queftion not, plenteous enough in it ; and
may be confpicuous to more judicious and lefs con-
cerned Eyes, though my own too fond ones may
not have been able hitherto to difcover them : In
which, as the Great V I R G I L himfelf found Gold
in the Drofs of E N N I U S, poffibly the moft cen-
forious and malevolent may own, that though there
are

arè fome * Lines and Paffages but *fo fo enough* of
àny ZoiLus' Confcience, a great many more may
be *tolerable* and *paffable*; — and fome *better* than
could be expected from fuch a *Country City* as is
Old E X E T E R.

I was launching, perhaps, into a too deep Pre-
fumption, and abafh'd draw back. — And yet, if
any one fhall think fit to attack, cavil at, or
banter it, or any the worft of it he can cull out,
let him but do it *fairly*, above-board, like a Man
confcious of his Ability, or righteoufly fo as it may
come duely to my Knowledge, and I will thank
him as for a Favour, however roughly, or fport-
fully (yet not abufively), handled by him. If he
condemns the Whole in Grofs, or any Part, it
feems but equitable he fhould *openly* fix upon Particulars, and affign Reafons, — in their Turn alfo
to be examin'd whether folid and of Force, or not;
— and whether indeed the *found Faults* may not
happen to lie in the *Finder.* Such fometimes
proves to be the Cafe. Some Wou'd-be Criticks
poffibly but *dream* that even minor Poets (or, if
you will fo have it, Poetafters) *nod.*

A Man is not, indeed, oblig'd to like a Thing;
and it may be juft enough in him to fay he does
not like it; — and that for the fubftantial and un-
anfwerable

---

* Alluding to *Sunt bona, funt quædam mediocra, funt
mala plura.*

anſwerable Reaſon, *becauſe be does not.* Let a Man be pleas'd at what him pleaſes. But alas ! to *prove* the Thing which he may have taken in his Head, or in his Will, to diſlike, (or, haply, has not in his Head whereby to like) to the Author's Face to be in Faćt condemnable, and give ſufficient Reaſons why no one elſe ought to like it, may not be ſo eaſy, or ſo ſafe. For the Tables might be turn'd upon him, and the Cauſe of his finding fault may be found to be either his own Malice or Ignorance, as well as Selfconceit, or Want of Judgment, Taſte, or Ingenuity.

If but in private only any abuſively treat this Endeavour to do good, as is too oft' the Cuſtom, ſuch clandeſtine Cenſure is pitiful and ſneaking, and is the Part of but *Scoundrels* in the true Senſe of the Word.

" Something two much, perhaps, of this " : For till I hear what Faults ſhall appear in, or be attributed to, the well - intended *Opuſculum,* much Apology ſeems needleſs, and hardly pertinent.

However,— a Word by way of Prevention, in one particular Reſpećt, may be requiſite. To aſſay a methodical Narrative of the whole (viſible) Tranſaćtion, I found a Neceſſity juſt a little to touch on the Appearance in it of our Worſhipful Superiors, The Time, the Deſign, the Nature, the facetious

Spirit

Spirit expectable in such a Poem, all, neceffarily
exacted a like jocular Style in this with what runs
through its other Parts. If the light Manner of
Expreffion may feem to over-fufpicious and fanciful Eyes to betoken an indecent Difrefpect in me
towards T H E M, fuch _Seem_ is a falfe Appearance.
I profefs a fincere Veneration for Legal Offices, and
all who worthily bear and maintain 'em. Neither
indeed hath the Mufe, though fhe may have been a
little familiar, and innocently playfome perhaps,
in the leaft whit been affronting, or even unman-
nerly. She has not taken a Tithe Part of the
Licence claim'd by, and allow'd to, others on like
Occafions. But even had fhe fallen with down-
right Invective on the Greateft among our Citizens
that acted fcandaloufly and bafely in their Stations,
fhe were by Reafon intirely juftifiable. " For
(fays the judicious Controvertift as well as mighty
Poet * M I L T O N) " though Men ought not to
" _fpeak evil of Dignities_ which are juft, yet no-
" thing hinders us to fpeak evil, as oft' as it is the
" Truth, of thofe who in their Dignities do evil.
" Thus did our S A V I O U R himfelf, J O H N the
" Baptift, and S T E P H E N the Martyr."

And fhould it be conjectur'd there were Inu-
endo's lurking of fome not over honourable Management, and fly Sneers at queer Foibles, in fome
few, even fuppos'd to be diftinguifh'd Perfonages,
                                                    it

* In his _Iconoclaftes._ Art. xv.

it might be anfwer'd, Some Faults and Oddities in fuch Perfonages may be exploded and fmiled at, and yet the inviolable Dignity of their Stations and Functions be heartily refpected. We know what is faid to the miftaken proud Afs bearing the Image of Isis, by the Kneelers but to the Goddefs, *Non tibi, fed Religioni* ; — Tis not to *Thee*, dull vain Animal, we pay this Adoration, but to the DIVI-NITY which thou, Porter, *bearest*. Befides, none but the *Confcious* and *Gall'd* can be *touch'd* by the poetic Lafh; — and that Lafh but tickles neither.

There may be Affairs carry'd on by but fome, perhaps a Majority, paffing in the Name of a Body Corporate, which others of them might utterly abhor, oppofe, and proteft againft. Such Gentle-men (for whom I cherifh a cordial Affection and Deference) I am confident, have more good Senfe and Good-nature than to conftrue in ill part the Points hinted at. And their Difpleafure alone in the Cafe would grieve me. They will eafily call to mind, in favour of my wonted Jocularity, that when the *CYNIC had in a grave Manner held forth againft the Vices of the City, and found that Peo-ple withdrew aloof, and kept almoft out of Ear-fhot, he began to tune his Throat, and fing in a pleafant Strain Part of a comic Song : Whereby he allured to him a confiderable Auditory, and gain'd Opportunity of declaiming againft their fa-

b   vourite

* DIOGENES.

vourite Foibles (though) in his wonted, humerous, more agreeable Way.

To write an Invective againft the reigning Follies of the Town, in a Mode and Style intirely morofe and ftern, would be far lefs efficacious than to do it in a Manner diverting withal, and in jocular though pompous Language. A bitter Prefcription may go down in a fweet Vehicle, which would be abfolutely refus'd, by moft Patients, if fimple and undifguis'd. Thefe Confiderations will, I truft, convince them of the Neceffity of the harmlefs Freedom taken, or rather with their Brethren, for the fake of others. As for the reft, —

"Why, let the ftrucken Deer go weep,
" The Hart ungalled play."

The random Verfe pretends to aim at no body. And if any body will, by crying out, declare himfelf an hit fome-body, no-body will pity him, but every-body laugh at him.

As for any coxcombic, proud, pitiful, Jacks in-Office, or " pelting petty Officers", carrying Bull-beef Grandeur in their Strut and Afpect, I fcorn to excufe my at any Time ridiculing fuch ftately Foppery. Pride is odious in any; but moft fo in fuch as can boaft of no Great Extraction, and of but mean Qualifications. The Pride of fuch is moft defpicable; its Emblem the fwelling little Reptile in the Fable.

, Perfons

Perfons remote, who may poffibly look over this little Piece of Rallery, may want to be advertis'd, That in the Time of the laft * Election of Members to reprefent this City in Parliament, one Party diftinguifh'd themfelves by Cockades of BLUE COLOUR or YELLOW. The Seat of one of the then chofen Members foon after becoming vacant, before it was known who would be Candidates for the Succeffion, the MOB (who before us'd to bawl about the Street, *Sound for* .... fuch an one: or *Sound for* .... fuch! — naming the Gentlemen) refolving moftly to ftick to their Leaders, or Alloers, in the foregoing Election, though intirely ignorant particularly for whom, chang'd their Notes to *Sound for the Blue!* and *Sound for the Yellow!* — meaning thereby they were refolute Retainers to fuch different Parties as had diftinguifhed themfelves by Ribons of thofe feveral Colours: And thence *the Blue* and *the Yellow* became the adopted Terms for *Tory* and *Whig*, &c. Thofe who efteem themfelves of the Better Sort prefently learning them, as well as the polite and genteel calling of *Sb-tfack!* of the Filth and Offscouring of the Kennel.

As MOBBING and Outrage are indeed but fuch, of whichfoever Side the Queftion, and fcandalous alike, I impartially diflike, and would equally explode, the bad Humour in *both*. But if

. b 2   it

---

* That which preceded the Mayoralty of Mr. ARTHUR CULME, which began in September 1737.

it be objected, that I ofteneft thus mention the *Blue*, I anfwer that I do it nothing in Proportion to the different Outcries made.

Nor let it be underftood as if I found fault with, or would ridicule, TRUE PATRIOTS — (as fuch among us there are, who aim the Publick Peace, and to prefer Worthy Perfons, whofe Wifh and Endeavour are the Welfare of the Nation, and of this City particularly ; — I fay, I would not have it thought that I in the leaft blame fuch) — for their moft ftrenuous Oppofition, in due Seafon, to a boifterous Faction. No. Nor can they, I think, be difcommended, of either Side, when M O B-BING is ply'd upon them to obftruct their lawful Proceedings, in Times of Choofing, for defending Themfelves and Rights, and repelling Force by *then* neceffary and juftifiable Force, even the like Force — defenfively. My goodnatured Satire bites, or rather gently nibbles, fuch only as are the *firft Mobbers*, or Raifers and Encouragers of *Mobs*, and fuch as perpetually belch out the difturbing Spirit of *Mobbing*, and abufe Paffengers or the Inhabitants, when they cannot feign the leaft Reafon for fo doing. The fame well-meaning Satire aims to fhame People, who would be difgufted to be reckon'd not of Gentility and Good Fafhion, not only from joining perfonally with, but alfo from abetting, or even tacitly and paffively counte-nancing, fuch Abominations in the prophane Rout.

ANDREW BRICE.

A SECOND
PREFACE,

Now in 1770.

THUS concluded the PREFACE writ more than Thirty Years ago. Haply such as are apt to " sleep, save under a Jig or a " Tale of ......, " may think it too prolix. Yet, as 'tis elucidating, as well as apologetic, it hopes from the Generous some Indulgence ; — we knowing not well to abridge it confiderably, but by abandoning the Performance to unjuft Sur-mifes. Favour may be the rather look'd for, in this Refpect, from the ample Compenfation made by my withdrawing fome Hundreds of Lines, pof-fibly many of the moft lufcious — [We mean not *obfcene*] — Lines, from the Poem itfelf, to reduce its Bulk, &c. However tedious the Prefatory Compartment be, fomething *additional* is ftill very requifite.

In

xiv. P R E F A C E.

In Anſwer to an inquiſitive many: That the
Poem was not forthwith, when compoſed, pub-
liſh'd, was principally owing to my being attack'd
with various intervening Maladies, and other very pitiable and forbidding Incidents, which had
ſet it by, ſcarcely at long length, remember'd.
Thoſe miſerable Circumſtances had quite overwhelm'd me long ere I conceiv'd an Idea of any
TOPOGRAPHIC DICTIONARY ; — that arduous
Undertaking, Labour inconceiveable, and Atten-
tion without Reſpite, which engroſs'd me whole!
In the midſt of which I was again ſuddenly flung
at the very Threſhold of Death's Door.

I err'd in ſaying *engroſs'd me whole:* For all the
ſame while the Management of my News-paper,
and *all* and *every* the Offices of a Maſter Printer,
Correƈtor, *&c. &c. whatſoever,* lay upon ſingle
me. I could ill be ſaid ever at all to *reſt*; for
when any ſhort Slumber ſhould have ſome little
eas'd my over - labour'd Thoughts, the D i c-
T I O N A R Y, that *Siſyphian* Toil! ſtill haunted me,
as bad perhaps as a perpetual *Ephialtes,* during near
Five Years together, without Relaxation.

Notwithſtanding all — (Be tributary Thanks de-
voutly offer'd *in the Higheſt,* and render'd here
below, * where ſecondarily due!) — I have *won-
derfully!*

* Namely to the worthy Mr. J. PATCH, ſtill living,
and my ſole ſurviving Helper. *O! ſero in cælum redeat!*

derfully! liv'd; nay, and liv'd to fee, and to rejoice in feeing, a very happy Alteration in Numbers
of the Common People. The more Confiderate
Sort growing afham'd of fuch horrible Mobbings,
the Populace have grown alfo lefs frequently riot-
ous, in natural very Confequence. Depriv'd of
the intoxicating *Swill*, heretofore lavifh'd in Profufion on 'em, to fet them outragioufly a madding,
in order to ferve no very laudable Purpofe, they
have become in *Fact* much foberer, in Defpite of
even any natural Propenfity to, or habitual Avidity
of, the annual Draff.

The Boys, whom I juftly ftyled the J u n i o r
M o b, and who bore fo brutal, fo fcandalous, a
Part in the Mobbing Tranfactions of the Day,
(and which latter were delineated, and painted
from the real very Life, in the Poem) have fince
that Time totally defifted from fuch abominable
and dangerous Practifes. Such their Reformation
may poffibly have been owing, in a meafure, to
better Tutorage, and ftricter Difcipline at School;
the Charity-Schools not excepted.

I with Pleafure, moreover, fee Reformation and
Improvement particularly in our Butchers; thofe
rugged *Chieftans* of the MOB in their *Old Days* of
Battle. They moftly prove at this Juncture very
different Perfons from thofe defcribed as in former
Times. Several of them now appear as polite in
Converfation at leaft as other Tradefmen, nor are
they

they at Elections more turbulent; on the contrary
their Countenances appear far lefs truculent at them
than heretofore they did. And, — Who could
ever have expected, Thirty Three Years ago,
that the Shambles would fo have produced a
R o s c i u s *(a)* for the Stage! —

I, for my own Part, (ever loth to offend) am
become full eafy in the *Publication* at *this* fo diftant
a Time from the *penning* of the Poem; in as much
as there remains alive not fo much as One Individual of thofe who were, in any refpect, glanced
at, or fatirically alluded to, in the pompoufly-ludi-
crous Touch-of-the-Time: — that blameable *Old
Time.* Nor is there one fingle Perfon NOW who
can reafonably think *himfelf* levell'd at thereby.
Such therefore as fhew themfelves touch'd will be
Funners of themfelves.

The M u s e indeed ingenuoufly owns, fhe de-
figned a flight fling, or fo, at fome *greatly offending* F E W. Nor *now* at all repents fhe. She
wrong'd neither of them in the fmalleft Tittle,
when fhe defcribed their ridiculous ftrutting Mien,
their fulfome fantaftic Behaviour, to fay no worfe,
at all Times. And, alas! did I but relate that
vile, cruel, yet fottifh, Attempt upon my very
Life, (entirely innocent and faultlefs in Deed,
Word,

(a) *Rofcius,* viz. Our worthy good Friend Mr. J o s.
F o o t.

Word, and Thought,) the Day, the *very mad*
Day, Twelve-month after the Æra of the Poem,
viz. in *Sept.* 1738, when the Mayoralty of Mr.
C u l m e was juſt upon its Expiration ; — by himſelf the ſaid Right Worſhipful, the then R-c-d-r,
and divers collected Aldermen ; and theſe goaded
on by Tertullus Secundus, of *Croak - Hum :*
All full of Fury : Subſerviently aided by a Poſſe of over-officious Conſtables, and *Mob-Conſtables*
for the Day : — I ſay, did I, as I might, fully detail
the vile Affair, Readers might cry Amazement !
at my uncommon Paſſivity, and think me indeed
Pidgeon-liver'd, in not having been adequately *ſe-*
vere upon them. But I pretty well expos'd their
headlong Doings, and ſatisfactorily aveng'd myſelf,
then forthwith, in my News-paper.

I particularly confeſs to have tipp'd a poetic
Fillip or two on ſome of the latterly mention'd
inferior Great Ones, at whoſe Head *march'd*, or
rather *pranced*, my worthy ſweet *Brother* G e o.
C - m - n g s : H E, who endeavour'd, by Wheedle,
to ſeduce my very Daughter, as H E *thought* and
deſign'd, to get her own Father *murder'd* in the
Name of *Law*. In ſetting forth his coxcombic
Air in the Ambulation to the Life, the M u s e
has aim'd at doing leſs than Juſtice : As all who
remember him will, I believe, amply teſtify. —
N. B. He being higheſt Bidder for the *Short*
Staff, or *Captainſhip* as call'd, procured the ſaid
Truncheon to be ornamentally tipp'd at each End
with Silver, and his Name, &c. engrav'd thereon.

c   Born,

Born, bred, brought up, and having always dwelt, in this City, I have a fort of natural Inclination to love her, as my Mother, and wifh fincerely for her Welfare. And having been well accepted, and in the main handfomly treated, from my puerile Days upward, by the Generality even of the Better Sort, I joyfully congratulate my worthy Townfmen on the happy Reformation of Behaviour that hath *in Part* already taken place, efpecially at Elections, — though not as yet to *all Perfection*, and fuch as, we hope, Time will gradually bring about.

And, oh! may this my playfome Satire, and jocular Rebuke, greatly conduce thereto!

During my poor Remains of Life I fhall heartily wifh a Continuance of Profperity, and growing Reputation, in all Refpects, to this my beloved native *E X E T E R* — (from which no Endeavours have prevail'd to draw me away) — till with all other Places fhe be, at laft, diffolved.

A N D R E W   B R I C E.

P. S. I beg it may be remember'd all along, that all the *Notes* and *Comments* were written at the fame Time with the *Poem* itfelf, except a few additional recent ones, for Diftinction's fake done in *Italics*, and included in Crotches [   ].

P R O E M.

PROEM.

HOW Lords defunct grow *Cherubs* may pertain
To reaching Bards, — who Heav'n explore,—
the Strain;
Who ken, with licens'd Eyes of glaring Hope,
Beyond the Stars, through Fancy's Telescope;
Puff'd by some feign'd URANIA to the Flight
Where *Rapture* bids the Things of *Sense* good-
night.
Be theirs with mercenary Fibs to treat
How Heav'n *respects the Persons* — of the
GREAT!
Worthies of virtuous Indigence — (For why
May *Virtue* not subsist with *Penury?*) —
Might nobly starving die, nor Half a Line
Canonize Them, or at their Fate repine.
To see *them* soar admits no sideling Glance
Towards the Poet's Pension or Advance;
Whilst Pimps to Pride by glav'ring Lays may
thrive,
Who praise the Dead — to flatter the Alive.

Not

Not Us by fuch Abuſe of Verſe behoves
To compliment vain Mortals up to Jo v e s ;
Though --(fram'd of an *unfaſhionable* Mood)--
We'd celebrate the ſcorn'd, brave, tatter'd,
     G o o d ;
Adore true Worth and Righteousness in
     Thrall,
And bow to M e r i t in an Hoſpital.

Be 't humble ours, impartial ours, to ſhew,
In earthly Rhime, Deeds viſible below.
Nor far let our *domeſtic Genius* roam,
Impuls'd to *(a)* chaunt but Vulgar Facts
     at Home :
Yet ſcorn, like *(b)* Bird in borrow'd Plumes,
     to grace
With pilfer'd Diction Thoughts of Common-
     place.
And may, if well ſucceeds our timely Aim,
More uſeful prove the low, the laic Theme.
We own it mean, — yet not of Matter poor;
Nor find the needed Subject ſung before.

(a) Alluding to Horace's   ——*Veſtigia Græca*
     Auſi deſerere, et celebrare domeſtica facta.

(b) Bird, &c. According to the Fable.

                               T H E

T H E

M O B I A D;
O R,
BATTLE OF THE VOICE.

C A N T O I.

OF Mobs, and Mifchiefs which from
      Mobbing fpring,
And pell-mell Battle of the Voice,
    I fing :
Nor that alone ; — for oft' the Conteft knows
Voice roughly feconded by Fifty Blows,
And Knocks more folid which hard *(c) Nod-
    dles* throw,
And Gripes and Tugs above, and Kicks below;
                Whilft,

(c) Noddles) Though *Noddle* properly fignifies but the
Occipitium, or Hinder-Part of the Head ; yet is it among
the Vulgar us'd for *the Head* entire ; but us'd indeed fomewhat contemptuoufly, like as a *Black Head*, a *Logger Head*,
&c. — the beft Heads in the World for Boxers, Bruifers,
and Cudgellers.

Whilſt, in *Cloſe Hugs*, clandeſtine Tooth and
Nail,
Unmanly, with diſhoneſt Wounds prevail;
That Scratches, Bumps, Black-Eyes, and Plai-
ſters worn,
Veſture beſmear'd with trickled Blood, and
torn,
Disjointed Thumbs, and many a feſter'd Scar,
Record the Fury of the baleful War.

This War, — this Gallimawfry of Debate,
Which I, — " Thing unattempted yet ! " —
relate,
This War owns Fellows-All, like Football
Play,
And, — as if All Mankind were of one Clay, —
Diſtinction quits, — that Offal Mumpers boaſt
Themſelves ſo good as Rulers of the Roaſt;
Makes Titles ſtoop, and with exalting Fire
Scrubs face a Knight, and Scoundrels ſide a
(d) 'Squire;

Levels

(d) Country Eſquires and Gentlemen having of late [*viz.
about the Time of writing this Poem*] very politely mingled
with the common Townſmen at Elections for Mayor, as
much as for Members of Parliament, as *honourary Freemen.*

Levels fix'd Merchants of Bale'd Staple Ware
With Merchants vagrant in a Peddling Fair;
Sets Ale-men, Alms-men, Aldermen, in Band,
Tight by each other, *brotherly*, to ſtand;
Makes Maſters liſt with Journeymen, and bears
Shopkeepers to take on with Garretteers;
Rebellious Sons, unnatural of Tongue,
Brave theirs, perverſly, from whoſe Loins they
  ſprung;
Flim-ſinew'd Taylors with a bluſt'ring Rage
Tarpawlings, bred in Tempeſts, to engage;
Saint-Methodiſts communicate in Din, —
Strange Coalition ! — with the Dead in Sin;
Smutch'd Colliers, armour'd in girt Horſehair
  Bags,
With mealy Millers to exchange their *Fags*;
Mean Oſtlers Big Innholders to oppoſe;
Lean Weavers dare fat Clothiers to the Noſe;
Spruce Valets cope gruff Grooms with rugged
  Noiſe,
And Learn'd Attorneys Clerks — rude 'Pren-
  tice Boys;
Makes Throats divine, whence Anthems ſoar
  on high,
Chime in with theirs who Rags or Rabbits cry;
           Makes

Makes floven Slaves who frowfy *(e)* Urine
 drive
With *(f)* Beaux who draw *Port*'s racy Wine
 to ftrive ;
Sweepers of Chimneys full prophanely rufh
On Sextons, who the holy Chancel brufh ;
Hod-bearers, and who trample *Cob,* to bawl
Againft their ferv'd Up-rearers of the Wall ;
Tinker his Powder black with Barber's white,
And Blood on Butcher, fcuffling, to unite ;
Brings Gatherers of Taxes loud to vie
With Gatherers of Afhes — to make Lie ;
Truft-needing, broke, Ha'penny-Pamphleteers
With hoftile Bawl bombard their Printers Ears ;
Debtors not dodge the *Bum*'s rapacious Paw,
Nor from ftern Beadle flinch poor *Rogues-by-*
 Law ;
Makes Juftice, warm'd, abet Sedition fell,
And Thief back a Companion Conftable ;
Them mingles who gauge Barrels, — or rid
 Bogs,
Command or School or Jail, — or ferve the
 Hogs ;
Dung-

<hr>

(e) Viz. to the Fulling-Mills, from the ftinking Abodes
of the Female Colle¢tors of it. *(f)* Tavern Drawers.

Dung-carriers, Cooks, and who Catharticks
   vend,   [mend;
Gems, Gewgaws, Grots; Bibles or Bellows
Subfift by Cards or Cocks, Heirs, Hurts, or
   Hops;   [Mops;
Make Coffins, *Crowds*, Malt, Marriages, or
Teach Birds or Witneffes; Eftates convey
Or Rubbifh; fmuggle, or watch Ships at Kay;
Cutters of Corks, Corns, Capers; Every Sort
And Size of Folk; fuch greedy War (in fhort)
As for Recruits craves Blind and Halt, nor fails
To rake the Hofpitals and fkim the Jails.
Yea, frail Inforcement Troops of Manhood
   glads
From crazy Dotards and yet callow Lads;
Worn wrifled Crones, green Girls, and mellow
   Maids,   [Aids;
Wives, Wh—, or Widows, ferve as fcolding
Unbreecheft Urchins lifp their puny Might,
And puling Chits fquall to affay the Fight.

A   ¶ True-

¶ True-humour'd Pow'r of righteous R I D I-
.   C U L E,
That jeers the idle Hurry of the Fool;
Brands Villains whom Laws reach not, as in
    'Game,
And sneers the Fop's Vainglory into Shame;
Religion's Hood from Hypocrites can steal,
And the false Patr'ot through his Mask reveal;
Degrade bad Ministers in Seats sublime,
And gibbet Judges, when unjust, in Rhime:
T H O U, --- who gav'st B U T L E R, in his
    H U D I B R A S,
To swinge the Whims of EACH fanatic Class;
B U T L E R, who cou'd with mimic Sportings
    tease,
Chide with a Smile, and with Correction please;
T H O U, --- who B O I L A U taught'st with
    facetious Taunt
Priests deadly Dudgeon for the *(g)* DESK to
    chaunt,
(Dudgeon, which made R O M E's ghostly
    Gluttons keep
Fasts uninjoin'd, and Sluggards baulk a Sleep)
                                        When

(g) In his Poem call'd The LUTRIN, in English *a Desk.*

When in a Saint's calm Chapple it befell
That *(b)* earthly Wrath with heav'nly Minds
   cou'd dwell,
Whilſt the proud Prelate curſt Revenge ex-
   preſs'd,
As he in ſolemn Prank the Chauntor bleſs'd :
Thou, who ſhew'd'ſt *(i)* Garth with
   Wit's poetic Mawl
On his own jarring Faculty to fall,
And frump ſage Warwick-Lane's tranſport-
   ing Feud,   [Blood,
Confeſſing *(k)* Poean's Sons the Sons of
That with unlicens'd Uſe of mortal Skill,
Whilſt ſcap'd the Stick, they'd one another
   kill ;
Kill without Phyſick, and, ſurpriſing ! ſee
Death-Pangs with Pleaſure, — though without
   a Fee :

            A 2   Thou,

(h) Anſwering to Virgil's *Tantæne animis cæleſtibus
iræ ?*

(i) Viz. in his Poem call'd The Dispensary.

(k) Poean, the Name of Apollo, properly as the
God or Father of Phyſicians.

THOU, CONCORD's Goddefs! Thou moft
   ufeful MUSE!
Me kindly to explode ·vile FACTION ufe,
Whom friendly Piques,~benevolent in Ire,
To fcoff down fhrewd, yet empty, SQUABLES
   fire !

   A Lancet-Pen, fet fweetly keen, prepare
For my Attempt, by thy conducting Care,
The Boil to ope with fuch chirurgic Art,
Its Point may tickle with a wholefome Smart !

   What might defpair the Pulpit, Bar, and
      Stage,   ⌈ Rage,
E'er to atchieve, though fhou'd combine their
May'ft THOU, by-ftanding, from the abler Prefs
Accomplifh with a Wonder of Succefs ! —
Since Sermons fail, let a Defcriptive Flout,
Held a reflecting Mirrour, bring about ;
With Raillery cut vicious Follies down,
And force to Laughter, to reform, the Town !

                    'TWAS

'Twas thus with Joke to honeſt *(l)* VULCAN
　giv'n
To reconcile an houſhold Brawl in Heav'n ;
Whoſe ſeaſon'd Check, divine Buffoon !— be-
　guil'd　　　　　　　　　　　　 [mild.
JOVE's Wrath, and turn'd ev'n Vixen JUNO
He limp'd to fill, with Mein of comic Sort,
The Peace-confirming Mazer of the Court.
Each boon Celeſtial quaff'd, in jovial Round,⎫
His brimful Bowl, with nappy Neƈtar crown'd, ⎬
And Party Heats in ſocial Pledgings drown'd.⎭

Help me rebuke, thus, our Inteſtine Fight
By painting it ridiculous to Sight :
Yet, though be drawn in ſtrong Groteſque the
　Strife,
Be all deſign'd and colour'd from the Life.
Good-natur'd the Intention, though ſevere
Sometimes our Verbal Piƈturings appear,
Who, --- ludicrous of Indignation, --- prove
Jocoſe in Cenſure, and inveigh in Love,
　　　　　　　　　　　　　　　And,

(*l*) VULCAN.) See HOM. *Iliad,* Book i. at the Con-
cluſion.

And, fcatt'ring Blame amid the blameful
 Throng,
Drub but with Drollery and fcourge in Song.

 Yet firft it's fitting we in Grief rehearfe
Our wretched Change in fome more ferious
 Verfe,
Led blind from *(m)* Wifdom's peaceful Paths
 aftray,
And pitch'd in Folly's deep difturbed Way,
Or headlong rufh'd from flighted Welfare's
 Height,
To plunge and flounder in a rueful Plight.

¶ In ALBION's Weft *erft* throve a Town
 (ere more
There MOBS prevail'd than *(n)* MONKS
 fo heretofore)
On which fair *(o)* ISCA fervile waits, whofe
 Site
NATURE to load with Dainties own'd Delight,
                                        And

 (m) Alluding to *Wifdom's Ways are Ways of Pleafant-
nefs, and all her Paths are Peace.*

 (n) *Exeter* was once fo over-run with Monafteries,
and the Vermin therein fed, that it obtain'd the Nickname
Monkton.

 (o) ISCA, or *Ifc,* the River now pronounced *Exe.*

And by *her* (*p*) Works fence'd from Annoys
to Health,

Whilſt with Home P L E N T Y vy'd Imported
W E A L T H :

For did its (*q*) Empory in Gain ſurpaſs,

Though now ſob we the Boaſt what Com-
merce *was !*

There *did* indulgent P E A C E (as Antients tell)

And gay G O O D - N E I G H B O U R H O O D, ſweet
Couple ! dwell.

N A T U R E to pamper yet abides ; but, ah !

Did friendly Love, off hiſs'd, with Trade
withdraw.

In ſtead, Spleen, Diſcord, and Contention, have

Flung murder'd Peace in an opprobrious
Grave,

Laid infamous Inſcriptions on her Tomb,

And voted Death eternal as her Doom.

That

(*p*) *Her Works.*) The City being naturally encompaſ-
ſed with Hills, which help to break the Force of injurious
Winds, &c.

(*q*) *Empory.*) The Woollen Manufacture and Trade
in former happy Days exceedingly flouriſh'd here in every
Branch of it.

That GOODWILL Angels pſalm'd from Heav'n
  of Yore
Is own'd our Duty and true Blifs no more.
Sweet Moderation's deem'd a ſneaking Sin,
A treach'rous Gate to let Deſtruction in ;
Whilft headſtrong Paſſion and a rampant Zeal
For ſtormy Nonfenfe aggrandize our Weal !

Hence ragged Penury hath feiz'd the Place,
And Defolation much deform'd its Face.
(r) Houfes, ſhut up, with difmal Fronts
  declare,
Unhop'd a Tenant or a patch'd Repair.
Yea fome, by Rats themfelves abandon'd, own,
Their tott'ring Symptoms, and for Ruin groan ;
Or faln, as if by the difgraceful Doom
Denounc'd in Scripture, Hills of Dung become,
Too like our *(s)* *Rock-Lane's* moft upbraiding
  Ground,
Where once were Charitable Manfions found,
On which lo ! Mountains of curft Rubbiſh rife,
To draw, like BABEL, Vengeance from the
  Skies.
                                        Hence

(r) [*Such really was the Cafe at the Time referr'd to,*
(in 1737 *&* 1738.) *when the Poem was moſtly wrote.*]

(s) [*The Complaint is now taken off.*]

Hence Induſtry, which, by a ſkilful Hand,
Adorns, and fortifies with Wealth, a Land,
Baulk'd and deſpis'd, ſcarce lives; or ſeems no
more
Than a mad Induſtry here to be poor.
Hence we to Swarms of cumbrous Idlers owe
Self-ſhaming Sighs, and Looks of guilty Woe,
Who might for worthy Bread with honeſt Joy
Their gainful Hands in proſper'd Arts imploy,
But that, with epidemic Itch o'er-run
For Mobbing, they the Means of thriving ſhun,
And vy in Labour to be moſt undone.

Be yet confeſs'd the Joy (nor let our Foes
Couch'd here a knaviſh Irony ſuppoſe)
That with our abject Dregs of Folk alone
Such begg'ring Fury holds a lawleſs Throne!
Joy that no RULER's Bent permits to fear
(t) A roaring Lion or a ranging Bear!

B No

(*t*) *Roaring Lion*, &c. See *Prov.* xxviii. 15.

No Turbulence of Soul can recommend
One who fhould to conferve the Calm afcend !
Nor Candor's deem'd, but by the Rafcal Race,
A Vice difqualifying for a Place !
No: Men of Poft the Way of Peace purfue,
Though rais'd in Uproar by a factious Crew !

But hourly we in Vulgar Converfe find
A froward Jargon harrows up the Mind.
One, ceafelefs, dull, coarfe Tintamar of Prates,
Fatiguing Senfe, a manly Hearing grates.
Thence due Complacence and humane Deport
Excluded are, or but receiv'd for Sport.

Contention which, when Night's illumin'd
    Queen
Was in twelve full re-borrow'd Luftres feen,
Here fought difturbing Reign by Law a Day,
Now through the Year affects diforder'd Sway,
More vile, more horrid, fhocks with frefh
    Alarms,
                                    [Arms.
And, reftlefs, keeps her Standing Troops to
                                ' In

In this frail Age of *Abſtinence!* when die

The Great — quick as the Little *bruſh away*,

And ſome One of our *(u)* Guardians Twice a
Score

Mounts on the Bleſſings of their feaſted Poor!

' That ſcarce a Month the Sky's bright Burghers
miſs

To welcome ſome juſt Steward to their Bliſs,

And hear th' Approbat from th' Empyrean
Throne,
                [done!

" Well haſt thou, good and faithful Servant,

And " Bleſſed, come; for Heav'n ſhall reim-
burſe,
                [Purſe!"

" With Gain, the Lendings of thy empty'd

ELECTIONS on ELECTIONS crowd ſo faſt,

A new begins ere a preceeding's paſt.

B 2   Such

(u) Guardians.) The Corporation of Guardians of the
Poor, Forty in Number. When one of the Number dies,
another is always to be elected in his ſtead; which Election
is ▲[*was at the Time here ſatiriz'd*]-- carry'd on, oftentimes,
with more Noiſe and Party Fury than in ſome Places perhaps that of Repreſentatives in Parliament.

Such chaunt we not, nor which in Senate gives

To fit the Town's *(x)* Twin Reprefentatives :

Sing we but what, in Annual Courfe, came on

The Day of Old devoted to the *(y)* M o o N,

When S o L Two Se'enights had oblique⎫
   his Chair ⎪
                   [Career, ⎬
Wheel'd fince from *(z)* Six to Six he made ⎪
With fainter Beams in our cool'd Hemifphere: ⎭

About that Tide when Geefe, in Panniers fquat,

Turn up alluring Shows of copious Fat :

That Day *(a)* when firft, enwrapp'd in flabby
     Rags,
                   [Oifter - Drags,
Our *(b)* S t a r c r o s s Mer-Maids caft their
                                     Whofe

(x) Two Reprefentatives for this City in Parliament.

(y) *Moon*, i. e. *Monday*, fo call'd from our Heathen Sax-on Anceftors on that Day worfhipping the Moon.

(z) *Six to Six*) viz. about a Fortnight fince Sept. 11, O.S.

(a) *That Day*) viz. the Monday before Michaelmas-Day.

(b) The fame Day on which we choofe our Mayor, the Oifter-Women of Starcrofs, &c. are allowed to begin drag-ging for Oifters.

Whofe fifhy Ends, hid in their modeft Boats,

Need not like Trowfers form their Petticoats:

That Year when Pilchards (*c*) to Our Betters
    fhew'd

Too plenteous to be *fafhionably* good,

With whom goes down no *cheaply-vulgar* Meat,

But (learn'd with artful Elegance to eat)

Force'd Viands praife, of recommending Coft,

When out of Kind, as out of Seafon, moft:

Year fince Diftillers wail'd the mulcted Sin

Which footh'd the Torture of the Guts with
    Gin,

Save when Two Gallons, fold exempt of Awe,

From crimelefs Cogues, as 'twere made drunk
    by Law.
                    [Spell

That Year when (*d*) Crux (as by Magician's

Ghofts dragg'd arife, but flip again to Hell)

                             Slunk

(c) Scarce ever within Memory were Pilchards fo plentiful and cheap in thefe Parts as in this Year 1737.---- Some of the Gentry efteem'd them a Nuifance.

(d) Treville Crofs, Efq; a certain half-mad half-fool
                                   'Squire,

Slunk from his *Manſion*-Jail with four Regret,
And choſe *for once* to pay the charging Debt;
But, ſick of nauſeous Creditors, agen
For Cure reclaim'd the Dun-defying Den.
That Year when in the fair Six-Gated Cloſe
To GOD devoted, (though there (*e*) MAM-
MON goes)
                                                    [aroſe.
As (*f*) Limes had fail'd, young thriving Elms

Yet ere arrives the critic Day, whereon
The FIGHT DECISIVE muſt be loſt or won,
                                                    Alehouſe

'Squire, of a very good Eſtate, who never caring to pay any-
body, ly'd perpetually in Jail : But at this Juncture fearing
the Act for the Relief ot Inſolvent Priſoners for Debt would
affect his Lands and Tenements, he paid the Debt he was
charg'd in Cuſtody for, and came out. Though he preſently
took care to return back to his ſaid beloved Habitation. Is
not ſuch an one a proper Object for Satire?

    (*e*) The Church-yard, where our Merchants, &c. &c.
aſſemble to talk of Trade and Buſineſs, &c.

    (*f*) Some Years after the prodigious great Storm in
1703, in room of the very large Elms which had been torn
up by the Roots, were Lime-Trees orderly planted ; but
not thriving, indeed gradually dying, Elms were, as at preſent, planted their Succeſſors, and flouriſh well.

Alehoufe Alarms, Street Camps, and Kennel
   Wars,
Prelude th' Heroi-Comi-Tragi-Farce.

Not brooking well wifh'd Time's too tardy
   Flight,
O'er Pipe and Quart, many a ling'ring Night,
With Fronts of Council, in important State,
Huge as of GERMANY th' ELECTORS mate.
Scarce paramount Receivers of Excife
Heap Royal Pelf in more majeftic Guife.
Scarce with a Swell of more judicious Look
Foremen of Juries kifs the Sacred Book.
Scarce Parifh-Warden, at an Eafter Feaft,
Nods Bigger, toafted by th' obliging Prieft.
The Baptift Saint fcarce at *Stich-Hall* may fee
More grand the Chiefs of Cabbage-Company.
Scarce a bluff Skipper, in his Realm of Wood,
Top'd up a petty Godhead of the Flood,
With kembo'd Arm, full Paunch, and bully
   Face,   [Grace.
O'er Punch-bowl fmoaks with more elated

                   Scarce

Scarce ftrolling Hero in Stage-Bufkins dreft,

Plum'd Helmet, ermin'd Robe, and gemmy
    Veft,

Between the Acts a mightier Afpect wears,

Whilft He upon the Candle-fnuffer fwears.

Nay, an Ale-Draper fcarce, — (who through
    the Bung
                                                    [Dung,
Once Barrels fcour'd of Dregs, fwept Stalls of

But now by Sots fo (g) *dam'd enrich'd* to deck

With Golden Chain his Heirefs Daughter's
    Neck)
                                                    [Pout
At Door, in cufhion'd Chair, with Grander

Extends his Cloath-Shoe Signal of the Gout.

Talk in Alliance future Deeds difplays,

And fcarce a Brag but which its Thoufand flays;

Or (where in common Room, oppos'd in Will,

Men, jumbled clofe, Mugs independent fwill)

                                                    At

(g) *Dam'd* is now by many us'd as the Superlative
Degree, as fignifying *very much*. My Meaning is, enrich'd
by difhoneft Means ; what is too common.

At Variance to a prefent Charge invites,
And bick'ring Boafts prove Overtures of Fights;
Loquacious Tongues in pellmell Clutter run,
As Breathings ere the Battle Main's begun.

Ale-houfes diftant vent their Clafh fo ftrong,
As if did all to one join'd Rout belong:
And yet diftinguifh we from whence and whom
Th' emphatic Twangs of boift'rous Babble come.

So, on th' Inauguration of a King,
When greater Six of our great Ten Bells ring,
Beyond the reft we note, each mighty Round,
The Cadence from huge (*h*) GRANDISON
refound.

PISTOL the Second flafhing Bounce lets off,
More furly render'd by a mingled Cough.
CULTER (*i*) (whom Shares of *liquid Bets* rejoice)
Sputters his dire Ferocity of Voice.

C   TESTY,

(*h*) *Grandifon,* from the Bifhop of that Name who gave
it, is the Name of the largeft of our Bells in Peal.
(*i*) *Ben. Cornifh,* the Cuttler.

T E S T Y, whofe Clamour fnarls, with Looks
afkew,

Holds forth as if he hallow'd for the *Blue* ;

Whilft (*k*) GLASSMAN, tamelefs by a Thoufand Bangs,

As bold a Clangour for the *Yellow* twangs.

THROUGHSTITCH (*l*) the faucy, who, each
Quart, outlies

All * *Philomaths* who ere mif-read the Skies,

And irritates correcting Fifts and Feet,

Is heard to bellow through a Mile of Street.

C A S T O R *(m)*, with creaking Words, half
fnuffled, brays

Odious as, wrangling, he at Cribbage plays :

Ne'er did a hamper'd Hog whine fo abhorr'd,

Nor Gelder's Clarion naftier Shriek afford.

SWIL-

(*k*) *Ingram* (the firft of the Family) the Glazier.

(*l*) *Throughflitch.*) This Spark had his Character drawn
long before this Time as --- ' A pert, noify, empty, prag-
matical, prefuming, impudent, contemptible, abominable,
Coxcomb, Lyar, &c. &c.

* *Philomaths.*) Almanack-makers.

(*m*) *B—ngh—m,* the Hatter.

SWILGALLON (*n*), lavifh of more Roar by half

Than APEWELL mimicking Owl, Afs, and Calf,

Blafts his big Organs in a deeper Key ⎫

Than Horns, and Hounds, and Bumpkins, ⎬
   raife, when they

With joint Cry open'd fcare the chaced Prey. ⎭

  Morn, Even, Noon, and intervening Hours,

Infulting Terrors now befiege our Doors.

Where'er ye turn, reproachful Flings ye meet,

And lubberly Affronts oppofe your Feet.

A currifh Growl, and a deep maftive Bark,

Bays you in Light, and follows in the Dark :

(o) H-a-a-a-h ! with Barbarity of Look gnarrs
   one,

Like Butcher's Dog o'er a defended Bone,

Plain in the Mufcles of whofe ruffian Face

The Wifh of bloody Maffacre ye trace :

C 2   Concerters

(n) Swilgallon. John St-v-ns.

. *(o) H-a-a-ah !)* They pronounce this ugly fpiteful *Hah*
with a rugged, harfh, grating fort of a Quaver, much
lengthen'd, like the arring or gnarring Growl of a great Dog.

Concerters run to back the odious Cry,

And, grinning, fnarl a furly Symphony.

Next flock grotefque around a faunt'ring Crew,

And perfecute you with *Sound for the Blue*!

Or fcarce lefs horribly your Patience wound

With like Annoyance, *For the Yellow found*!

Confus'd you compafs, leap with dafhing Pace,

And yelp foul Jeers with impudent Grimace;

With flourifh'd Felts, perhaps fkin-deep, affail

Your Face, and rankling leave a ghaftly Ail.

Though paffive ye mute expedite your Way,

Outrage obfcene will after you inveigh.

Nay, thankful be if ye fo clean evade,

Nor more material Peft'rings cannonade.

When no flain Cat, Clout, Shoe, nor Filth
    advance,

Salute yourfelves the Favorites of Chance;

Bleft if you flip their fcarifying Claws,

Or fcape expectorated Shot from Jaws.

Sing Laud in Rapture, if unkick'd your Shin,

Though fpatter'd, ftinking, drips entire of Skin.

View

View with Delight your footed Hat compound

For Coat's not fweeping, with You dragg'd,
the Ground.

Nay, if o'ercaft, for Miracle record
                [gor'd:

That Ye arife nor bruis'd, ftamp'd, punch'd nor

And hymn Te Deum, as for Life's Return,

If a fore-grip'd, not ftrangled, Throat ye mourn.

                              [forbear

What though fome Topping Vulgar may

In Perfon to affaffinate your Ear,

Too often they fuborn th' Inferior Mob

With vaffal Rage you of your Peace to rob:

With hir'd Sedition they direct the Broil,

And pay in Drink the Wages of the Toil.

So thofe whom Maftives combating delight,

To ftimulate them to the fangy Fight,

Stroke firft their hardy Loins, then to purfue

With fervile Barkings cry Alloo! Alloo!
                  [Fray,

And, when they have fuftain'd the prompted

Spit in their Mouths the filthy liquid Pay.

End of the firft Canto.

CANTO II.

AT length that *(a)* Monday which the
Day preceeds,
                                        [ty Deeds,
When prais'd the brave *(b)* Arch-Angel's dough-
Heav'n's Captain, by whofe Loyal Army fell
The Rebel Legions, now the Thralls of Hell;
While poor and thoughtful Tenants fore lament
The fad Defects of the laft Quarter's Rent,
And mortgage Gown, Sheet, Rug, and Difh,
     to blefs
Bed, *Crock*, and ufeful Pitcher, from Diftrefs;
That joyous Monday, dawning in the Skies,
Awakes pert Gladnefs in th' Electors Eyes.
                                        Whip !

(a) Monday. viz. the Monday before the Feaft of *St.*
Michael, appointed the Day for the Choice of a new Mayor.
   (b) Arch-Angel.   St. MICHAEL.   See the Service for
the Day, &c. &c.

Whip! the moſt forward bolt unbutton'd out,

And, kenning, throw their partial Looks about;

Then, joining, to Diſcourſe o'er canvaſs'd owe

Prognoſticks how the Day's Affair will go :

And where the Doors firſt ope for Tipple's Sale,

Time's Forelock feizing, *ſwig* courageous Ale.

Now Kitchen-Maids, knock'd up by *Chu-*
rers (c), ſtretch

Unready Limbs, and Sighs of Envy fetch.

The Stage-Coach Porter, malapert of Tone,

Swears Jehu, long-ſince ready, will be gone:

The up-ſcar'd Paſſenger brief Stay implores;

And yet an Hour the drunken Jolter ſnores.

With owly Eyes the ſtrolling *Seekers* ſkulk,

And hopeful peer at Stall, Porch, Door, and
Bulk.
    [hold

The clean Diſchargers, with rince'd *Cools* be-

Stoln back — as if aſham'd of —*finding Gold.*

            See!

(c) Churers.) So in *Exeter* are called. thoſe in *London*
ſtyl'd *Chair-women.*

See! chafte Aurora grows with Blufhes red
Efpying Phoebus fprung from Tethys' Bed,
Or fkitting Cats from am'rous Scratchings come,
Or naughty 'Prentices flunk drowfy home.
The Drummer, on high *(d)* Rugemont's
    crumbling Mound,
Beats ftrong the bold Revelle's roufing Sound.
Whiftling to River waggles Groom on Steed ;
And Milkmaids jocund to Teat-tugging fpeed.
The Scavenger drags on his rumbling Carr ;
And Centry's led to guard the Chief of War.

The Sixth Hour Bell with venerable Knoll
Bids Wakers mind — or Body or the Soul :
This World's Folk *up*, and wordly Work
    attend ;
And t'other's to celeftial Bus'nefs bend.

Tilers

.*(d)* The Hill on which our Caftle ftands, and in which
the Regiments, at Times, quarter'd in this City keep Guard,
is called Rugemont, from the Rednefs of the Earth. [I
think, beating the *Revelle*, we know not why, has of latter
Years been difus'd.]

Tilers and Masons by their Briskness show,

They idly to no whole Day's Labour go.

Taylors, not *franchis'd,* with a loit'ring Gait,

Till Bell rings (*e*) quick, before *King's - Alley*

wait.

It rings: They shrugging budge a lazy Pace,

And o'er the Shoulder turn a grudging Face.

It rings: The faintly few who feel the Mood,

And Liberty, and Leisure, to *be good,*

With Lips in Form to Duty set, and Eye

Fraught with Religion's Glance, to (*f*) Mattins

hie.

Handmaids behold, who have, in *Cold* of Day,

The pious Orders proxywise to pray,

Whose Ladies indispos'd,— by Sloth,— a-bed,

Depute 'em to act heav'nly in their stead,

D   On

(*e*) At Six o'Clock a Bell knolls, or tolls, for Prayers, at the Cathedral; then a Bell rings quick to give Notice that Prayers are about to begin. [In King's Alley, at the Time of writing this Poem, liv'd 3 or 4 Master Taylors of principal Business.]

(*f*) Mattins. Morning Prayer.

On Pattins trip,— with fanctimonious Charms;

Starch'd *(g)* clainly neat, with Pray'r-books
   under Arms.

                             [drawn,
Young *(h)* Choirifters, from Neft reluctant

To Worfhip truant, *force'd Devotion* yawn.

But Voices voluntier make fhift to raife,

By Organs though unaided, worthier Praife,

Lefs artificial Praife, while in the Soul

Heav'n may hear *Melody (i)*, tho' Voices growl.

The *(k)* Pile of venerable Grandeur round ⎫
                                            ⎪
Emits the folemn Tune : Th' enclofed ⎬
   (l) Ground   ⎪
                                            ⎪
Anew feems hallow'd by the facred Sound. ⎭

But whence that Noife prophane ? Whence
   that fhrill Shout,

Which impioufly quells the Din devout ?

                                     The

(g) Cleanly neat. Like HORACE's *fimplex munditiis.*

(h) Chorifters. The young Singing Boys.

(i) Melody.) Eph. v. 19. *Making Melody in your Hearts*
to GOD.

(k) Pile, &c. St. Peter's Cathedral Church.

(l) Enclofed Ground. St. Peter's Clofe.

(m) The JUNIOR MOB fonorous ufher in

Their Claim of Pelting, and lewd Rites begin,

Whofe bufy Sholes ranfack'd the Common-
fhore,

And rummag'd Dungheaps, for a batt'ring Store.

Hog might in vain feek with fagacious Snout

Apples worm-eaten or corrupt to rout.

D 2   Did

(m) Junior Mob.] The Boys. Our true-born Citizens
are (Numbers of 'em) train'd up to *Mobbing* from their
Cradles. To the Praife of fuch a polifh'd People as we are,
our well-bred *Infantry* are permitted to fling Turneps,
Potatoes, Pieces of Cabbage-ftalks, &c. at the poor Countrymen whofe Bufinefs brings them into City this unlucky
Morning: At whofe Approach the young Mifchiefs, running to meet 'em, fet up a Cry of *A Brother! A Brother!*
A Brother! and fall a battering of them immediately. If
one offer to rebuke them, (as I once prefum'd to do, and
had like thereby to have brought not only them, but fome
Loggerheads of the Shops, upon my own Back) they daringly
reply'd, *'Tis lawlefs Day! 'Tis lawlefs Day!* And fo indeed might it be imagin'd, while fuch barbarous Outrages
(as feveral others at different Times, fuch as the Dafhing
up the Kennel-Water on Paffengers, which they call Strat-
ting, &c.) are not only tolerated in Effect, but laugh'd at,
and thereby encourag'd. With Indignation I remember a
poor Man had one of his Eyes thus actually on the Spot
ftruck out by one *Butler*, who afterwards attempted with
others to fire the Deanry-Houfe, &c. So they grow up
to Villainy by Degrees.--- *Nemo repente fit turpiffimus.*

Did pregnant Sows for out-caſt Onions long,

The grunting Mothers, ſick, might caſt their
    Young.

Each plunder'd Gutter void of Turnip rills,

Nor it a Carrot, or Potatoe, fills.

For theſe ere HESPERUS, with brilliant Light,

Led ſlowly on the laſt impatient Night,

The YOUNG INIQUITIES had ſpuddling found;

Arms from aloof by miſſive Force to wound.

Parſnips and Cabbage-ſtalks, to handy Size

Cut up, glad with augmented Store their Eyes.

The Ammunition ſwells each Pocket ſtrout,

And each Hand bears the Surpluſage about,

Till Clown, miſled by ſome malicious Star,

Yare by the Strippling Poſſe kenn'd afar,

And met beyond the mid-way Diſtance, grows

Th' aſtonied Handſel of their volant Blows.

Sharp Clamour from their Throats in Concert
    rings,

And ev'ry Hand a Root, ſcarce erring, flings.

A

A Brother! Brother! they exulting cry;

And Show'rs, full Tempeft, quick repeated, fly.

Repeated? Yea, at a contiguous Rate

The Flingings whiftle an inceffant Threat.

Not half fo frequent noifome Ware is known

On Perjur'd Heads thro' Penance Loophole
    thrown;

Ev'n though fuch vile detefted Heads pertain

To the paid Rafcals of th' Informing Train.

Lefs numerous a white long Winter fpies

From glowing Hands hard-kneaded Snowballs
    rife,
                    [BIRTH

And Truncheons, hurl'd to folemnize the

DIVINE, maul (*n*) Cocks lefs fwift with
    murd'rous Mirth.

                              As

(*n*) *Cocks.*] To the Credit of Parents, Mafters, Conftables, and other Overfeers, ought it to be over and over
mention'd, 'till the deteftable Nufance ceafes, that the very
wicked Diverfion [*Horrible! that the* Human *Nature can
ever be diverted with* Inhumanity] of Throwing at Cocks,
which other wheres, I think, is thus moft barbaroufly practifed but on Shrove-Tuefdays, not only continues here the
whole Chriftmas *holy* Days, but commences fome Weeks
before them. It's obfervable too that fome of thofe who are
the greateft Sticklers for what they call *celebrating* the folemn
                                 Feftival,

As he difcovers, ftagger'd and aghaft,

On Him alone the frolick Mifchief caft,

Bleak Horror thrills his Veins, a qualmy Damp

In his chill'd Bofom quails the vital Lamp :

The ruddy Brown his burnt Complexion fails,

And Palenefs o'er its freckled Flufh prevails.

His 'wilder'd Thought ' Whence his Offence'
inquires,

What Rage this *Infantry of Belial* fires?

Why is, by the Adult, the Youngfter Crowd,

He ponders, thus to (*o*) *gallow Folk* allow'd ?

To *gallow* ? Yea to gaul, perchance to lay

Folk fprawling, or by worfe Mifchance to flay?

To

Feftival, too much countenance this horrible Pollution of it.
For Shame, ye Parents ! For Shame, ye School-mafters.
And why fhould I not fay, For Shame, ye Magiftrates, &c. ?
It's recorded of *Diogenes,* the Cynick, that feeing a Boy
commit a Fault, he ran at his Mafter, and ftriking him faid,
Wherefore are your Scholars not better taught ?

(*o*) *Gallow Folk.*] This being ftill ---[viz. *at the Time
fpoke of*]--- a *Devonfhire* Word, though from SHAKESPEAR
it feems to have formerly been generally *Englifh,* implying
to fright, fcare, or aftonifh, is, I hope with Propriety
enough put into the Mouth of a Devonfhire Ploughman, &c.
We feem to continue the Ufe of the Word in that of *Gallows,* or *Gallow-Tree,* fignifying the Terrifying Tree, or
Tree of Terror.

Were Bacon Sows in Years too ſtricken found?

Did Pig yield up the Ghoſt without a Wound?

Or grow by Art in ſopy Wrapper fair?

Were Eggs ſold addle, or confounded dear?

Did *Chanticleer*, of Threeſcore Broods the Sire,

A cruel Length of Drop by Drop expire,

Then, lopp'd of Spurs, and circumcis'd of Comb,

Look beauteous in young Fowl of Turkey's [room?

Had breeding Geeſe, ſucceſſive Ten Years ſhorn,

Their Teeth-proof Hides, to paſs for youthy, torn?

Was Butter ſtamp'd to hide Defect of Weight?

Would *Doll* a' ſtroaking, or a' churning, ſnite?

Such Guilt was *Dame's* and *Doll's*; and but infers

They could out-wit o'erweening (*p*) *Citiners.*

To

(*p*) *Citiners.*] So, alias ſometimes *Zitiners*, many of our neighbouring Country People name us Citizens; whom they are proud to *out wit*, that is in plain *Engliſh* to *cheat*, in a Bargain. It's but little to be doubted Pigs and Poultry which died a *natural* or *accidental* Death have been ſold to us. I've been under the Roſe inform'd by a Farmer's Wife it's common

mon

To *Meafter's* Score ought to be chalk'd the Sin
Of Faggots fmall, and fappy green, led in:
Him, him alone, fhou'd Malediction fmite,
When, *ftifling* puff'd, they fmoulder, loth to
 light,
Who, teaz'd for Rent, permits their faulty Mirth
Whilft, finging, they with Froath befpawl the
 Hearth.

Dame, Doll, and *Meafter,* finning,—let pertain
To *them* to expiate with fuited Pain ;
But, for *himfelf,* he ruminates, and through
Finds Confcience clear of Crime, tho' whelm'd
 by Woe.

Then why fhou'd Innocence unholpen wail,
And wicked Pranks againft the Juft prevail ?
He little learns from the licentious Bray,
Commixt with *Brother ! Lawlefs, lawlefs Day !*

Around

mon to wrap up Pigs in fopy Cloths, to make their Skins
caft white.   Some of the other Tricks I have myfelf known
practifed ; particularly a very fuperannuated Cock, manag'd
as in the Text, fold for a young Turkey.

Around the fportive fierce Tormentors crowd,

Each to excel in Pranks mifchievous proud.

He wiftly turns for Help imploring View,

Cits rural born, made Denizens, on You !

But, fleering pitilefs, ye rather chear

The Onfet, and the cruel Paftime fhare.

Ungracious, evil-minded Town ! Had THRACE

For fuch a (q) PONEROPOLIS *a Place?*

Might he revolve in anguifh'd Heart, had he

Been fchool'd in Letters and *Greek* Hiftory.

With wretched Baulk he'd *trow,* Attacks
   fo hot

Might foon expend the Vegetable-Shot :

For ah ! as they difcharge, the fcrambling Bands

Quick recolleft the Shot with greedy Hands,

E   Which

(q) Poneropolis.] That is to fay an *Evil City*, or rather
a City of Wicked Ones. " We read (fays Monf. Bayle,
Diff. Vol. 5. pa. 789. *Lond.* Edition) " that *Philip* ga-
" ther'd together the moft wicked and incorrigible Men
" of his Time, whom he lodged together in a City he built
" for them, and call'd it *Poneropolis.*" It ftood in *Thrace.*

Which feem more folid, and alert, to bound,

Like thrown (r) ANTÆUS ftrengthen'd by the
Ground.

Brickbats and Stones deficient thefe fupply,

And on him heavier Flings of Evil try.

Were Dung with thofe to fail, and Lemon-
fkins,

Huckfters for Pillage hold vaft Magazines.

The Hind fobs difmal deep.   Sobs nought⌉
    avail : |
                         [Belly wail ⎬
Back, Sides, Breaft, Shoulders, Neck, Hips, |
Their joint Contufion by the pepp'ring Hail. ⌋

His Pate, inclin'd beneath lopp'd Hat, to fave

The Face, may foon a Cap of Plaifters crave.

His drooped Sconce fmart Ruins clatt'ring
    thwack,
                         [of Back.
Thence with continued Stains pollute his Length

                                   Cheefe,

(r) *Antæus,* &c.) The Giant whom (according to the
Fable) HERCULES encounter'd, who, as often as he was
thrown, receiv'd frefh and greater Strength from his *Mother*
the *Earth.*

Cheefe, dry'd obdurate, in his ftoreful Poke,
And Bread of Barley, crumble at the Stroke;
Or batter'd the brown ftony Walls of Pye
(Tho' firm as a Redoubt) in Fragments lye;
Or Pudding, which did Gobs of Suet teach
Confolidation, dafh'd, admits a Breach;
Or dangling Key's from trufty Purfe-ftring torn,
Or Sheath in twain from Knife, in Trowfers
  born.

By *Civil Pow'rs* abandon'd to Diftrefs,
Shou'd mifer'ant he *Agreftic Gods* addrefs?
Alas! old PAN's no more; SYLVANUS fleeps;
Nor chriflen'd BRITAIN a POMONA keeps;
Long fince the DRYADS left to haunt the
  Grove,
And tripping FAUNI ceas'd the Lawns to rove.
And cou'd fuch Godlins hear him, they'd retain
The Boon, till they might opportunely daign
Him *ruftic Vengeance* in fome pathlefs Clofe,
Glade, plough'd Land, Greenwood, or the
  prickly Gofs;

E 2   Where

Where might juſt (*s*) *Wherrets, Scats,* and
   Whiſterpoops,

Reap Satisfaction on the *truant* Troops,

When, *(t) Michers,* they for Neſt, hedge-
   breaking gò,
                                    [Sloe.
Or (*u*) Oackcub, Haw, Blackberry, Hep, or

Wou'd venting *Bitches Whelps!* revenge his
   Smart,

Or belching *Whoreſon Brats!* aſſert his Part?

Correction, by ſome plaguy Left-Hand flung,

The Scandal ſtrikes abortive off his Tongue.

Wou'd Geſture threat? Vindictive Hurls more
   thick

Will ſcarce afford him Space to brandiſh Stick.

And ſhou'd it drive, he'd turn'd the Slingers fee

Offend, like PARTHIANS, in a Feint to flee.

                                    So

(*s*) *Wherrets, Scats,* &c.] Country Words for *Blows,* &c.

(*t*) *Michers*] or *Truants.* Shakeſpear uſes the Word in
his HEN. 4.

(*u*) *Oakcub.*] So the People in Exeter call the *Chaffer,*
probably from that Inſect's pitching on *Oaks,* and feeding
ou the Leaves.

So rife the Balls pufh on their airy Run,
They nearly cloud like rifing Mifts the Sun.
Nor guiltlefs of at leaft a bloodlefs Wound
The fleet Offences from the Mark rebound.

Gall bids him bann : To bann affays he vain ;
A Dafh on Mouth dings back the Curfe again.
Confound! and direr Words, were his ; but, footh,
Gore damms the Sound gufh'd from up-rooted
    Tooth.
Back on himfelf the execrable Vote
Recoils, and wreaks harfh Rigour on his Throat.
But had he vex'd ELISHA's dooming Breath,
Which drove on Pefts lefs nocent mangling
    Death,
                [wou'd draw,
His feller Mood whole GREENLAND's Bears
Nor one devoted Caitiff 'fcape a rending Paw.

He weeps, morofely weeps ; and fee ! o'top
His heaving Breaft big Tears of Anger drop.
But Tears the Rocky melt not, rather Tears
Work their triumphant more offending Jeers.

As

As o'er his blubber'd Cheeks Eyes bootlefs gleet,
His Whine for Mercy duns the giggling Street.
But oh ! -th' Inexorable ! were as well
To (*x*) Adders, as relenting, urg'd the Yell :
For as, when Military Felons jaunt
With Backs flead raw, the long long (*y*) *Lope*
   of Gaunt,
Drums ruff big Rumble, in exerted Rowls,
To over-roar their Pity-craving Howls,
So Shouts, predominant of Noife, unite
To drown the Yawling of the pefter'd Wight.

Since, then, in Flight alone Afyle he hopes,
Through the flagitious Rout he hobbling lopes.
              Before

(*x*) *Adders.*] The Word, fay Criticks, ought (with the *Septuagint* and the *Vulgate*) to have been render'd *Afp*, which in Pfalm lviii. is called *Adder.* and faid to be *deaf*, and to *ftop his Ears*, fo as not to hearken to the Voice of the Charmer ; it being confidently affured that this Species of Serpents actually fo ftop their Ears.

(*y*) *Gaunt.*] Meaning that Martial Punifhment call'd *Running the Gaunt lope*, as invented or ufed firft at *Gaunt*, or *Ghent*, in *Flanders.*

Before him tofs his focial Tits in Fright,

Nor need commanding (*z*) *Rhee! Terrup!* or
    Hight!
                          ⌈Steel

Struck Flints cut Sparkles from the clinking

That hobnails o'er or clouts his ample Heel.

The loadfome Clog attempted Hafte impedes,

And, fliding, baulks th' induftrious clumfy
    Treads.
                             ⌈fcour;

Yet could high Trot the fcamp'ring Bumpkin

Hard after would purfuing Mifchief pour;

Nor, till he gain'd the Gate, Relief he'd gain,⎫

If, by ill Fate induc'd, no recent Swain   ⎬

Should intercept the Brunt of mafiy Rain.   ⎭

    Beware, raw (*a*) Pagans! who, in Morning's
        Prime,

Bring Grain or Wood, or fetch manuring Lime,

                      Beware,

(*z*) *Rhee!* &c.] Thefe are Terms or Sounds us'd by
our Country Wood-carriers, &c. to command their Horfes by, to go forward, to turn or incline to the Right-hand
or Left. *Terup*, I imagine is as much as if to fay, *Troop*
along!

  (*a*) *Pagan*] This Word in its genuine and original Im-

Beware, nor enter, though by lawfull Calls,
On *lawlefs Days*, th' inhofpitable Walls,
Left fhould demolifh'd Nofe, loft Tooth or Eye,
Your Paffage through our Civic Highway buy.

port, means no more than *Villager*, or *Country-man.* But
taking it even in its prefent common Ufe and fecondary
Senfe, might it not have been fomewhat incongruous to have
reprefented him as apt to call on the fictitious *Rural Gods*
without making him poetically a Sort of Mifcreant or Heathen ? Neither is it uncommon to fay of our Country Pa-
rifhes that they are but *a Parcel of Heathens*, --- though
many of them behave more *chriftianly* than many, or indeed
the major Part, of our Citizens.

End of the Second Canto.

CANTO III.

CANTO III.

SCENES ſo perplex'd in juſt Aray to bring,
And regularly of Confuſion ſing,

Proceed, O MUSE! in Order, to deſcribe

The various Actings of th' Electing Tribe;

From thoſe who marr to thoſe who muſter
Votes,

Aid by (*a*) *well-wiſhing*, or well waſhing Throats;

Club Voice gratuitous, or, wiſer, fell,

Aſſiſt by drinking or by drubbing well;

Thoſe who, to regulate the Stir, — (*as far*

As Law directs) — with Staves of Peace make
war;

Or only bribe, or only bet, or bawl,

Debate in Houſe, or domineer in Hall.

F At

(*a*) *Well-wiſhing.*] Such as are not *Freemen*, but as being
Well-wiſhers (as they call it) to the Cauſe are allow'd of
each Side intitled to the *Quill*, provided they bawl well.

At hand's the Hour when Nymphs in
    Screams acute

Deep Entries for the Vent of Milk falute;

And PETROCK's Tow'r, with added *(b)* Head
    fublime,

[Chime,

Since Day-fpring firft ftrikes up *(c) religious*

Pfalmy the Notes; — though, haply, in a Pet

Did STERNHOLD them to fnip-fnap Mufick fet.

Shrill *(d)* Hautboys and the fhriller Trumpet
    greet,

Attentive Ears, by Turn, in ev'ry Street;

Whofe

(b) Added Head.] A fmall Dome, or Turret, being
lately built o'top of it for the Reception of another (I think
a fixth) little Bell.

(c) Religious Chime.] At 8, 12, and 4 o'Clock, St.
Petrock's Chimes play STERNHOLD's queer *old Tune* of the
Fourth Pfalm.

(d) Hautboys, &c.] The City Waits and Trumpet,
about this Hour of Eight, begin to traverfe the Town, and,
after a Flourifh or Tune, their Spokefman, one of them,
fummons the Free-men, to the Purport of the Speech here
fet forth in Verfe, in thefe following very Words :---" The
Right Worfhipful ---- [Here a little Paufe] ---- " the
Mayor of this City, ---- [Here another fhort Paufe is made,
and off they *almoft* pull their Hats] --- " The King's Majefty's Lieutenant, &c. &c. &c.

Whofe Warble ceas'd, the Prolocutor hems,

Hauks, fpits, and annual Edict thus proclaims:

" The Worfhipful this City's May'r, " [*A*

Paufe

Moft gracefully here interrupts the Claufe.]

" Lieutenant of His Majefty the King,"

[*Here Hands to Hats full mannerly they bring.*]

" Hereby commands all Free-Men to prepare

" To choofe a new one for th' enfuing Year.

" God fave the King ! " — Thus toot th' har-

monious Band,

And mouth the Mandate, at each ufual Stand.

Glad Routs of Little Ones their Hafte- purfue,

As if *(e) pide Pipers* ftrange Inchantment

blew.

F 2   But

(*e*) *Pide Pipers.*] If any are ignorant of the fo fam'd Story
of the Rat-charming *pied Piper*, who drew 131 Children
after him out of the Town of HAMEL, in *Germany*, and
with them enter'd a Mountain that open'd to receive them,
they may read it afferted for real Fact in VERSTEGAN'S
Antiq. chap. 3. [*I now in 1770 add, it may be feen in my*
Topogr. Dict. *Art.* HAMEL.]

Yet why that manifold, that mingled *(f)*
Whoop?
                                        [Troop ?
Why jump in Confluence yon' ſtruggling
With prying Eyes, Muſe ! haſten to explore
Whence the wild Hurry, why ſuch early Roar ?

In Street intitled *High*, by the fam'd *(g)* Lane
To Venus ſacred, ſtands a ſacred Fane,

                                        Though

(f) Yet why, &c.] Betimes this Morning ſome generous
Zealots of the Pariſh of St. *Laurence* caus'd a Hogſhead of
Cyder, for the Uſe (if it ought not rather to be call'd *Abuſe*)
of the Populace, to be brought, and its Head placed, near
the Centre, cloſe home to the Church-Wall ; over which,
on a Pole fix'd to one of the Buttrices, was diſplay'd a blue
Apron for a Flag ; whilſt on the Tower hung another *Apron*
of the ſame Colour, adjoining the wither'd Limb of an Oak
Tree, ſtuck up, according to their *ſingular* Cuſtom, the
Twenty Ninth of *May*. While the Mob were filthily
draining the Veſſel happen'd the Rev. Mr. W------
(Whatchecum) to ride by ; on whom ſome of them fell
with affronting Language, Hollowings, indecent Geſture,
&c &c.

(g) Lane.] Caſtle-Lane in the *Highſtreet*, as infamous
---[*formerly*]--- for Drabbing, &c. as was ever the Suburra
of antient Rome, or are *Drury-Lane* of London, or *Damnation-Alley* (as 'tis nicknam'd) of Plymouth. ---['*Tis farfrom ſuch now in* 1770. *Inſtead, a very ſpacious, commodious,
eaſy Road is now made or making from the Highſtreet up home
to the Caſtle.*]

Though graven Images and Shields, *ere while*

Forming a (*h*) Conduit-houfe, its Porch com-
pile.
　　　　　　　　　　　　⌈mocks

Its Window, beautious, (Thanks to Lime, that

With Freeftone Afpect red and rugged Rocks)

To fanciful Obfervers feem to fmile

That Nature's Works its paffive Side defile.

Smile they?— But — hift! —. —

Ought we but tell, that (void of (*i*) guardful
Pale,
　　　　　　　　　　　　⌈Stale,

To fend againft lewd Dog's or Drunkard's

　　　　　　　　　　　　And

(*h*) *Conduit.*] Before this Church heretofore ftood a Conduit, which being pull'd down, of the Stones thereof (carv'd
with the Image of Q. *Elizabeth*, as I think it is defign'd to
to be underftood, Coats Armoury, &c.) was built the prefent Church-Porch. But whether they have been addition-
ally confecrated or not I find not in *Izacke's* Memorials of
Exeter.

(*i*) *Guardful Pale.*] It's a *ftinking Shame* that, for Want
of proper Palifades or Rails, this Church's Side is made a
perfect Jakes of. If this facetioufly fatircal but true Defcription, &c. fhall provoke proper Perfons to amend the
Fault, my End and Drift will be in great meafure anfwer'd,
who have not Patience to fee the *Houfe of God* thus irreve-
rently pifs'd upon, and worfe. *Procul, o procul efte pro-
phani.*

And poftern Sinks, by Night, their Stain more
vile)
[Pile,
Here ftands (ah! why prophan'd?) a rev'rend
Infcrib'd to Saint who dy'd, the Legend faith,
A *(k)* grilliaded Martyr of the Faith.

The Dons who in this confecrated Dome,
When in the Mood, to folemn Duty come,
Vow'd, in a gen'rous Ardour of the Heart,
Unparallel'd to top Election's Part ;
Yet cheaply noble, in Profufion wife,
Save Charge of Malt, Hops, Brewage, and
Excife.

So, — at the thrifty Coft of *(l) Twelvers* Nine,
Is Hogfhead bought replete with Apple-Wine.
Ere Bakers, to appeafe the maund'ring Maw,
Their foremoft Batch of reeking Manchets draw,

The

(k) A grilliaded Martyr.] St. LAURENCE, as *The Golden
Legend* tells us, being martyr'd on a Sort of Gridiron, or
Iron Hurdle, when half broiled, call'd to the Officer who
prefided at the Execution, telling him one Side was dreft
enough, therefore he might turn him up, and begin to fall to.

(l) Twelvers Nine) The Price of a Hogfhead of Cyder
was *Nine Shillings* or thereabout, at the Time of this Tranfaction.

The Orchard's Juice arrives, with fluid Song,
And dances as it flashing jolts along.
The liquid Hurliburly in the Butt
Portends its troublous Rumble in the Gut,
Whose Lee's foul Pother intimates as plain
The deſtin'd Perturbation of the Brain.

The Bells (whoſe Match no Carrier's Fore-
Horſe e'er
Could, for capacious Size, preſume to wear)
Their tinging Clappers, tripple Clink, imploy,
And ding-dong wrangle forth parochial Joy:
The trebble Diſcord peals exact the ſame
To 'wail in doleful Claſh a Houſe in Flame;
Nor more prepoſterous they'd wayward ring,
If did they quarrel to burleſque the Thing.

From

(m) *Bells.*] The Tower, built of red roughiſh Stone,
being much larger than, though ſcarce ſo high as, many
Chimnies, it's eaſy to ſuppoſe its Three Bells (for there are
full ſo many) claſhing make moſt excellent Muſick. A
Country Boy paſſing with his Mother a while ſince by, and
obſerving the Tower, innocently cry'd out, " *Look, look,
Mother, what a gurt* [great] *Chimley that little Houſe hath
got!* "

From the rough Tow'r (which late a Ruſtic
(*m*) Youth

Suppos'd a Chimney of enormous Growth)

An azure Enſign on a Mopſtick waves

Its hoſtile Flutter, and to Battle braves :

It lately had with faſten'd Strings embrac'd

A (*n*) purſie Ale-mans' Bulkineſs of Waiſt.

Behold ! an Oak's Branch near, whoſe wither'd
Spray

With Verdure ſhone laſt Twenty-Ninth of May.

Might not the Change the Patron's Gall provoke,

His ſprightly (*o*) Laurel for the faded Oak ?

No; Him delights ſuch Badge of ſturdy Love,

That to (*p*) APOLLO's adds the Tree of JOVE.

This Pennant ſcouls Defiance.   But below

Its brother Pennant flaps inviting Show,

The

(*m*) See the Note juſt preceding.

(*n*) *I think the dropſical Aleman* TOM JOICE.]

(*o*) *Laurel.*] The Etymology of LAURENTIUS is *Laurum tenens,* i. e. *Holding the Laurel;* as the prefatory Introduction of his Story in the *Legenda Aurea* gives it.

(*p*) *Apollo's Tree,* &c.] The *Laurel* is ſacred to APOLLO, as is the *Oak* to JUPITER.

'The hemm'd blue Linen, fix'd to Buttrice, flys,
And looks a-drying hung to Strangers Eyes :
But errs the Guefs ; for lo ! its Signal's plain,
To fwill and leak, and fwill and leak again.

Beneath this Poll, which, ftay'd, the Banner
    ftays,
The Cafk an Angle of the Prop inlays :
Snug at the Centre of the Temple's Wall
The Veffel's Head is *help'd*, or *helps*, from *Fall*.
Oh ! that we could the knotty Symbol cleave,
And obvious to the Light the Meaning leave,
If it implies — That *Toping*, in a fort,
Should *prop* the *Church*, or from *Her* have
    Support !
But we, dilemma'd, and in Search too flow,
Permit to thofe fage Emblemifts to know,
Who thus ordain'd the Manage, what in Mind
By fuch odd Difpofition they defign'd.
The Mob of clear Pretenfion rife draw near,
And fpring to feize Intoxication's Share.

G   Th'

Th' increafing Many burn with rival Thirft,

And new Intruders elbow back the firft.

The Faucet's (*q*) Regent (for, as in the Eaft,

Of Old were chofen Ruîers of the Feaft,

One governs here the Tap) rifks now the Fate

Of the (*r*) fquafh'd Steward at SAMARIA's Gate.

Matrons *(s)* of TRULLA's Kin, in Rags, among

The bowfing Tumult, *For Blue!* fquealing,

throng.

Girls, with Boy Tyroes for the Caufe, wedge in

The medley Quaffers, and unlearn to fpin,

Who, early thus taught Modefty to lofe,

Scarce in their Teens feek Bufinefs in the Stews.

Imagine

(*q*) *Faucet's Regent.*] One *Lewis*, a Journeyman of Mr.
Wills, Chair-maker, was appointed to draw the Liquor, or
at leaft to fee that *no Wafte* was made thereof,--- that is to
fay that none but the *right-colour'd* Mob devilify'd themfelves therewith.

(*r*) *Squafh'd Steward.*] See II. Kings, vii. 19, 20.

(*s*) *Trulla.*] The Virago, or mafculine filthy Jade,
brought in by the Poet among the Mob at Bear-baiting in
Hudibras. There have been feveral of them too much encourag'd here.

Imagine now that Point of Day when
(*t*) JAMES

By Bell's Ring warns devout-and-dainty Dames,

There fcarce are Sixty Minutes more allow'd

For humble Worfhip to be trick'd up proud:

The Point when, licking Butter from their
Bread,

In clean Frocks neat to School are Children led;

Whilft fav'ry Steams Nofe to folicite rife

From the fupp'd Liquor of cry'd Mutton-Pies,

And lufcious Clamours oft' regale the Ears

With Hot bak'd Apples! or Hot-fmoaking Pears!

When (*u*) LORD SINPIOUS, wrung with penal
Gout,
[rubb'd out,

Since Houfhold Pray'r, which had Old Score

G 2   Had

(*t*) *James.*] JAMES MORTIMORE, the honeft old Bell-toller and Chime-ringer. The Time here by Circumftances defcribed fignifies it's being now Nine o'Clock.

(*u*) *Lord Sinpious.*] The nicknam'd Lord at South without. Father *Dod*, I remember, has among his printed *Sayings* " Either *Prayer* will make a Man give over *finning*, or *Sin* will make him give over *praying.*" But this praying and fwearing, godly and wicked, heavenly and wordly-minded Inftance helps to confirm that there's fcarce a *general Rule without an Exception.*

Had let a Thoufand Execrations fly,
And ran anew in deep Debt to the Sky.

Now fcatter'd Parties, Drove confronting
    Drove,
With thwartive Eyes adverfe in Mixture move.
Here Helliers ftraggle in a lazy Shape,
As, flouching, they with Hands in Pockets trape,
Or thruft below their Aprons, fplafh'd with
    White,
Patch'd, furl'd, or dangling clouterly to Sight.
Crifpinians, flippant, though of fturdy Air,
More blithe, and with a galliard Pace, go there.
There hie who drew from (x) TUBAL - CAIN
    their Race,
                                        [Face,
With Copper Brightnefs glows each well-ale'd
There limp grim MULCIBER's befmutted Kind,
Their forgy Throats with quenchlefs Sparkles
    lin'd.

                                        Here

. (x) *Tubal-Cain.*] He is faid to be *an Inftructor of every
Artificer in Brafs,* &c. Gen. iv. 22.

Here Carpenters fhew Backs of ample Square,

Like knurly Beams rough-hewn of Oaken Ware.

There Barbers hop with Brows knit politic;

Here (*y*) Mafons, ruddy as their Cheeks were Brick.

Combers, in Veft by Ufe refin'd, and Oil

All fplendid, fhuffle to the lov'd Turmoil.

Here tinctur'd Hands diftinguifh thofe who Dye;

There Fullers fcud, perfum'd with Chamber Lye.

The greafy Frock of Candle-dipper there

Infpires near Noftrils with a fatter Air;

Whilft to a Feaft the fnuff'd grofs Odour craves

Our Houfhold Vermin from their Planchent Caves,

That, if befriended not by Pufs, their Foe,

Gnawn (*z*) HATTO's Fate he'd, haply, undergo.

Taylors, now each a Man, with nimble Trip,

Aping a jauntee Mein, there, fwagg'ring fkip,

Whofe

(*y*) *Mafons.*] Mere Bricklayers are in *Exeter* ftyl'd *Mafons.*

(*z*) *Hatto's Fate.*] HATTO, a vile Archbifhop of *Mentz* is faid, or rather *forg'd*, to have been eaten up alive by Rats, a Judgment on him for calling the Poor Rats, &c. &c.

Whofe Hearts feel fcarce more aggrandizing
Swells
                                    [Bells,
When their hir'd *(a)* Text conforts the hireling
Or while on *(b)* Bridge at Iron-Dish they ftand
In Vifit to their own wall'd Gallows-Land.

Scarce could they wear Looks more fuperbly
    fierce,

Was each a Bowhay or a Bully -- ARSE.

Gad Bakers there, whofe fweaty Caps, beneath

Hats meal'd and dough'd, their fcorch'd brown
    Temples wreath.

Here Flocks of Weavers, who this Morn difdain

Their Beechen Bowls of Broath new vamp'd to
    drain,

                                    Keen-

(a) *Text.*] On *Midfummcr-Day,* when the *Exonian Tay-*
lors chufe a Mafter of their Company, they fignalize themfelves, beyond other ordinary Corporations, by hiring a *Ser-*
mon to be preached before them, --[of which one heretofore
had the Text *Let him that hath ftolen fteal no more,* --- and
another --- *Yet a Remnant fhall be fav'd*]-- and the Cathedral Bells to ring all Day.

(b) *Bridge.*] The Burial-Yard of Heavitree-Gallows be-
longs to our Company of Taylors to take care of, for which
a Bit of Land was bequeath'd to 'em. Once a Year they
walk out in a Body to vifit it, when on the Bridge, at a Place
call'd *Iron-Difh* they tarry fome Time, treating each Paffer-
by with a Mug of Ale.

Keen-ey'd, alert, clank (as they huddled walk,
All Tongue, no Ear) harſh Vehemence of Talk:

Like Maſh of Jabber flooded (*c*) Exe beſtows,
When ruffled ſhe o'er rugged Head-Were
flows.

Grum Catchpoles, arm'd with Oak-Plants,
huge of Knob,
Indulging Vacance from a Harpy Jobb,
Among the reſt with itching Claws reſort,
And with a mingled Terror daſh the Sport.
Thoſe too who drive th' o'erloaden Sledge ad-
vance
With hagard and outragious Countenance,
Whoſe Laſh Laſh Laſh incarnate Fiends diſplay
On the hard, cruel, killing (*d*) Steep of Kay.

Slaves

(*c*) *Exe.*] The River on which *Exeter* is ſituate, and
from which that City derives its Name. *Head-Were* is the
Name given to the uppermoſt of the Two above the Water-
Engine.

(*d*) *Steep of Kay.*] *Kay-Hill.* England is ſaid to be a
Hell for Horſes. If ſo, this Hill may be call'd *Kay-Hell.*
Hereon a Perſon of tender Humanity, and a ſympathiſing
Goodnature,

(*e*) Slaves of the Shambles, with more ugly Low

Than ere they learn'd of madded Ox or Cow,

Loud, fwift, and foul, as Torrents roaring down

O'er (*f*) *Stepcote-hill,* that rage *Exe-Bridge* to
    drown;

Where-ere the fanguinary Ruffains roam,

The Jaws of licens'd Slaughter feems to foam.

But why is thus Detail in Special made?

In Sum, we fee large Draughts from ev'ry Trade,

As they in feparate Brigades go by,

Or jumbled mifcellaneous in Allie.

Street, Lane, and Alley their Contingents fend,

And ev'ry Tap-Houfe yawns for Dividend.
                                        Deft

Goodnature, may too often be ftruck with Horror. Surely
it were not very difficult to evince, by Reafon and Scripture, that the harden'd Wretches who ufe God's Creatures
with Cruelty, or lafh them on to Performances beyond their
Strength, fhould expect to anfwer for it hereafter, as for
Sins unnatural. [*This Hill hath been made a little more prac-
ticable.*]

(*e*) Slaves, &c. Journeymen Butchers, fuch as *Afbly,* &c.

(*f*) *Stepcote-hill.*] To the Weft of this City is a Defcent
call'd *Step-cote-hill,* to which as the Butcherow leads, the
Guts, Blood, Litter, Ordure, and a Variety of Naftinefs
from the Shambles, are, in hard Showers of Rain, rapidly
carried over it into the River, juft by *Exe-bridge.*

Deft Managers, betimes, with fearchful Care,
Smoak Who are Who, as fundry Signs declare,
As cunning Spies to reconnoitre fcout,
And fteal Advice what lurks the Foe about.

Now Chiefs of haughty Bofom fupple ftoop
Ev'n to the Jakes to angle for a Dupe,
Who for a Wheadle will invert his Coat,
Or for a Promife proftitute his Throat.
The Mafter-Tradefmen courtly condefcend
To call a fimple Working-Man *my Friend*,
Familiar fit, and pledge, by touching Pots,
Whom they have fkunn'd for Scoundrels,
      Scrubs, and Sots.
A tatter'd *Gaffer* is accofted, *Sur !*
And *Shabs* are *Neighbours* own'd without De-
      mur.
Druggift to Pounder tips obliging Wink,
And Mercer afks his Errand-Man to drink.
Grocer on Porter's Arm lays fweet'ning Pat,
And Draper to a Taylor touches Hat.

A Small - Ware - Man extends his plumper
 Hand
To fhake a Pedlar's ; And, upwheadled grand,
A Tinker to a Goldfmith cover'd goes ;
And Merchant greets Japanner of his Shoes.
Nay, Parifh Clarks, who rev'rend Surplice wear,
And whofe *Affent* authentic renders Pray'r,
Whom (box'd in hallow'd Defk, full Jole by
 Cheek
With Parfon) Learn'd in Look, demurely fleek,
Reading a clear Half-Title to the Gown,
We muft (g) *Inferior Clergy!* duely own ; —
Ev'n Clarks lay by their State, and Sextons join,
As they co-equal tope, co-equal Chat and Coin.
STARTUP, magnificent of Thought, though He
Adorns in Pew Chief-Warden's big Degree,
His wonted Infolence forgoes a while,
And nods a Congee with a lureing Smile.

CELSUS

(g) *Inferior Clergy.*) So a certain Clark in this City ftyl'd
himfelf and his brother Clarks. We (fays he) of the inferior
Clergy can, fome of us, read better than our Mafters.

Celsus the folemn, whofe *Plutonian* Frown
Looks fupercilious on mere Mortals down,
Affumes a Spice of almoft civil Guife,
And bears a Dafh of Sweetnefs in his Eyes.
(h) Pumilio, whofe all-penetrating Sight
Through the proverbial Millftone meets the
    Light,
Great on the Bench as Hudibras is fung,
(Where, formidable for a doubty Tongue,
With Him not *(i)* Abel on the Stage com-
    pares
In bearing up th' *Importance of Affairs*)
Not wanted yet at Council-board to fpeech,
Sits clofe Companion with fome vulgar Breech.
Ev'n bulky *(k)* Tuber, whofe vaft Stomach
    fwells
Much as the Fable of the *Paddock* tells,

H 2   And

(h) Pumilio, alias *Dandiprat.*
(i) Abel in the Play call'd *The Committee*, &c.
(k) Tuber. [*I knew this Perfon doubtlefs in* 1737, *but forget him now in* 1770.]

And more the Cloak, fo late put on, dilates
Than an High-Mighty of the *Belgic* States,
Abate an Inch of bloted Grandeur can,
Nor look immenfer than an Alderman.

Though thefe Patricians fcatter Vows to fight
Like Roman Tribunes for Plebeian Right,
And promiffory Patriots become
As popular Love-winning ABSALOM,
Yet MOBS true-fteel'd and ftomachful reject
The ftale Cajole, nor will defert their Sect.
Defert their Sect?—As foon a Jilt fhall rap
A flufh'd new Cully for a fleec'd old Chap.
As foon the Spark fhall keep Connubial Vows
Who makes, for Pelf, a leathfome Crone his
    Spoufe :
Curmudgeons hate of free Regales to tafte,
And Girls in pamper'd Idlenefs be chafte :
They Horns efcape who Youth at Sev'nty wife;
And Vintners Riches with their Grandfons
    thrieve :

Upftarts

Upſtarts in Office more obliging grow,

And on the Outed Proofs of Love beſtow.

CLODIUS leave Wenching, to oblige his Wife,

And TABID Toping to preſerve his Life :

As ſoon ſhall *(l)* PHILL the prideleſs ceaſe to tell
[befell,

What Things when he *Head - Steward* was

Or what Events took place in ſome great Hour,

Whilſt dignify'd He Chair of Governour.

Deſert their Sect ? What ! turn a Recreant ?

No ; ſooner be incurr'd of Bread the Want.

No ; they, tenacious of their proper Dyes,

Propos'd Cockades of alien Hue deſpiſe,

And, firm as Rocks, by Tides ne'er overborn,

In Love of Privilege, known Welfare ſcorn.

Nay, ſome, more moody, their own Maſters beard,

And piſh at being from Imploy caſhier'd ;

Ill

(l) PHILL. PHILL BASTARD, who in all Companies lugg'd in ſomething to ſpeak of his having been one of the annual Stewards, or Bailiffs ; and the ſame with regard of having had his Turn of being Governor among the incorporated Guardians of the Poor.

Ill Names retort, and dafh Upbraidings by,
And Serjeants menac'd to the Back defy.

Thus ftout ST. PETER elevates his Tow'rs,
Expos'd to Thunder, Stormy Blafts and Show'rs;
But ftands them all unmov'd, and braves the Sky
To fpend its Rage in conftant Battery;
Seems but to whiftle at the Wind; the Rain⎫
Precipitates with Scorn; and with Difdain ⎪
Hears the wroth Tempeft beat his founding ⎬
    Plain.   ⎭

Ale-foakers now exert their leachy Skill
Quick to induce the *(m) Running of the Quill.*

                           Shall

(m) Running of the Quill.) When the Rabble have Liquor given 'em before, at, or after Elections, they fay *the Quill runs* at fuch or fuch a Houfe; and they getting themfelves drunk by it they call *Quilling*, or drinking upon *the Quill*. I conjecture it had its Origin from a *Quill's* being us'd for the Liquor's *running* through from the Mefhing-Vat in Brewing. Nor is it indeed impoffible but a *Quill* was heretofore us'd here inftead of a modern Brafs Cock, or Wooden Faucet; we ftill faying *Put the Jug,* &c. *to Pen,* when we'd fignify the having it *run* from the Hogfhead immediately into the Jug.

Shall to be *freely drunk* the *Right* be loft,

That beft of annual Rights Shab-Freemen boaft?

Rather come on no free Election more,

Nor ev'n the prided Privilege to roar!

For Parties both, amidft their Jarrs, unite

In Claim to fhare the Bacchanalian Right.

No Quill run? Rather Flood-fwoln Exe away

Run with the *Ifland* Malt-houfe to the Sea!

Let (*n*) Bangs on Stalls, and jollier Wickednefs,⎫

Hoots, Drabbing, Fiddling, Swearing, Cavils, ⎪

ceafe, ⎬
      [Prince of Peace. ⎪

And Brabbles, on the Morn when born the⎭,

Yea rather let each new-chofe May'r detain

The City's Buckets; let the Butchers chain

           Their

(*n*) *Bangs*, &c.] The Chriftmas-Day Morning is moft fcandaloufly abufed here by the Particulars above-mentioned, and a hellifh Variety of other Wickednefs and Outrage. Mean while, fome accompanied with Fiddles, others without them, rove about the City, and under Windows fing Carols of Chrift, God, and the Holy-Ghoft, and fo make them in Deed the *Song* of the *Drunkard*. And for fuch impudent Prophanenefs they are rewarded, having not only *Chriftmas Drink*, but Money to be more drunk with, given 'em. —[*But fuch fcandalous Night-Mobbings, &c. &c. have of later Years been much fupprefs'd and nearly quafh'd.*]

Their Maftives up, in Spite, to difannul

That glorious *Law* of *worrying a Bull* ;

And fo — preventing mortal Colds by Sweat,

Or Colds as killing by (*o*) Affaults of Wet) —

Reduce the wonted Flufh of Deadly Trade

Of thofe who wield the Peftle or the Spade.

But oh ! in vain they fkilful Mumpings ply ;

For yet the Chiefs their *Running Quill* deny ;

And Tefters, here and there, ftruck up, fuffice

But juft a heart'ning Quart or fo to raife.

Yet Patience, Soakers ! and forbear to dun :

Quills fhall as freely as the Conduit run. —

As ponded Mill-Brooks, free'd of Bar, redeem

Loft Time by gufhing in a rapid Stream,

Anon, in Seafon, though Stagnation now

Witholds the Current, fhall Ale-Rivers flow.

What

(o) *Wet.*] The Butchers, &c. who are annually permitted to beat a Bull (a Diverfion which too many of our tender-
hearted fine Dames feem to delight in) before the Mayor's
Door, throw Buckets or Hats-full of Water on all they can
reach, &c.—See another Note on the Occafion in Canto iv.

What though ALPHEUS (*p*) hides awhile from
　View,
And feems to bid his upper Banks Adieu,
Frefh, frefh, in Vigour, he breaks forth again,
And vifibly flows jocund to the Main.

(*p*) *Alpheus.*] This River doth run quite through *Arca-dia*, *Elis*, and along the City of *Pifa* ; foon after which it is fwallowed up in the Earth. From thence it is fuppos'd to run, by a fubterraneous Channel, under the Sea, without mixing with the Salt Water, and fo to pafs quite into *Sicily*, where it mixes itfelf with the Fountain *Arethufa*, near the City of *Syracufe* ; infomuch that any Thing that is thrown into it on the *Elis* Side is faid to come out of the Fountain above-named. Vid. Diod. Paufan. et al. Hence the poetic Fiction of *Alpheus*'s Love to *Arethufa*. Univ. Hift. Vol. ii. pa. (fol. Edit.) 406. Note (b).

End of the Third Canto.

I　　　　　　　　　CANTO IV.

CANTO IV.

BY this, where Houſes, whelving, Houſes
    meet,

And vault with Beetle-brows a ſhelving Street,

Where ſtout *(a)* St. PETER, on the Corner Stall,

Props the impending Edifice from Fall, —

The luſcious Smoke of Furmity an Hour

Had tempted errant Younglings to devour.

By this had Rural Blowzes made their Rounds,

On Steeds-and-Panniers, in the licens'd Bounds,

Whom grudg'd Half-penny's Fee admits to⎤
    ſcream   ⎟
                    [Cream, ⎟
Milk, Cabbage, Apples, Butter, Eggs, and⎬
And *(b)* OTHO made their Malediction's⎟
    Theme.   ⎦

                                  By

   (a) St. Peter, &c.] Meaning *Northgate-ſtreet.*
   (b) Otho.] Mr. OTHO CHANNON, the Market-Man,
and my honeſt Kinſman.

By this had funky *(c)* JENKIN, Friends prefume,

Of Pipe the tenth whiff'd the white curling

Fume.

[harangued

By this had *(d)* SKINDLY through ten Streets

With lewd loud Scandal, and been voted hang'd.

By this hiftoric SNARL thrice tenthly fpake

His Faculty of — Pronenefs to — *miflake.*

By this did SORDID, Lip-bewraying, ftuff

His Noftrils with his fiftieth Gripe of Snuff.

I 2 By

(c) Jenkin.] JENKIN WILLIAMS, the honeft *Welch* Landlord of our Eaftern *White Hart* Inn, fo tight a Friend to the Revenue, that is, fuch a perpetual Smoaker, that he feems, in fome Meafure, as if he fubfifted partly by it: For which Reafon Wags have affign'd to fuch his Smoke the Epithet of *vital.* He is an early Stirrer, and fticks the Tube in his Jaws, as foon as (if not before) he fteps out of Bed; from whence he fcarce ever plucks it but to fill. Suppofing him to have gat up, this Morning of extraordinary Bufinefs, between Five or Six, we can't in Confcience allow him lefs than his *tenth Pipe* by Ten o'Clock. An hyperbolical Fellow once offer'd to maintain, by a moderate Computation, he had Fire enough in his Pipe during the common Six Days, if collected into a Body, to boil his Pot o'Sunday.

(d) Skinley.] The moft noify and moft fcandalous of R--fc--s, whofe chief or only Delight was induftrioufly to fpread Defamation, falfe or true, through the Town.

By this hail *(e)* CHAMPION, like TITHONUS
bleſt

In early ſhaking off unhealthy Reſt,

Had on ten Benches try'd whoſe Ale was beſt.

By this had the Eccleſiaſtic Chime

Proclaim'd of Forenoon-Pray'r the inſtant Time;

Whilſt Nymphs not prink'd-up with Ball Airs
to pray

Sat ſipping Slander with their Pagan Tea.

By this, another Morn, had *(f)* Drum been
heard

[Guard,
With martial Beat to chear the marching

Nor were the Warriour Wags array'd to play,

In Garriſon kept ſafe from Warfare's Way,

And mock the Town-Imployment of the Day.

But

(e) Champion.] Mr. CHAMPION, of the *Swan* Inn.
He is truly deſcribed in the Verſe.

(f) Drum.] Preciſely at Ten was wont a Party of the
Regiment quarter'd here to march to the Caſtle, to mount
and relieve the Guard. But, of late, ſince Mobbing run
ſo high, the Commanding Officers, to prevent the Soldiery's
interfering with, or being drawn into, the Squabbles of the
Town, have us'd to order 'em betimes into the ſaid Caſtle;
where

But whence that Hurricane of Voice we
hear?
[appear!

See! Crowds in Deluge through EASTGATE

The Yellow (*g*) GREEKS with vaſt Huzza
ruſh in;

And Blues look bluer at the dauntful Din.

For leſs intrepid and ſecure of Fame

The gen'rous ROMANS of the (*h*) FABIAN Name,

March'd

---

where being confined all Day they have us'd to divert themſelves and Officers with a Mock-*Election* of their own,
which they have ſometimes done very comically, one Party
being for the Time reputed *Blue*, the other *Yellow*, &c.

(*g*) *Greeks.*] So we Surname, I know not why, the rugged Inhabitants of St. *Sidwells*. The Title ſeems to have
ariſen from their contending with the City at Foot-ball, &c.
they being call'd *Greeks* as making the Invaſion, and the
Townſmen perhaps *Trojans* in defending their Ground,
&c.

(*h*) *Fabian.*] Near about the Year of *Rome* 280. *Cæſo
Fabius* and *T. Virginius* being Conſuls, the Plebeians refuſing
to inliſt to ſerve againſt the *Hetrurians*, who invaded their
Country, the *Fabii*, to the Number of 306, with about
4000 Vaſſals and Clients, generouſly engag'd to ſecure the
Frontiers againſt the Enemy. They march'd gallantly
through the Gate *Carmentalis*; which became famous thereby; but which, on their being to a Man cut off, was afterwards nam'd *Porta ſcelerata*, or *the accurſed Gate.* See
Ovid Faſt. l. ii. --- *Carmentis portæ dextra*, &c.

March'd through their fam'd CARMENTAL
   GATE, to go
And quell the Infults of th' HETRURIAN Foe.

As under *(i)* SHALLDOWN's cliffy Coaſt,
   where TEING
                                       [Spring,
With Brine confounds, at Ebb, her fwœeter
When NEPTUNE drives the mobbing Flood
   along,
The liquid Ridges turbulently throng,
Waves hilling on the Backs of Waves fwell high,
And on the craggy Upland throw the Spry,
Then in her Bay ufurp the leſſ'ning Strands,
And roll an Ocean o'er the ſhelly Sands,
So the rough Populace, in-guſh'd, amain
Extends on each Side of the paved Plain.

                                   Three

(i) Shalldown] A little Fiſhing-Town, between which
and *Teignmouth* runs the River *Ting*, or *Teing*; or rather
where that River difembogues. The Defcription of the
Place and of the Tide's flowing there is exactly natural,
whether or no it be artfully enough poetical. Nor, we hum-
bly prefume, is the Simile or Comparifon quite unapt.

Three ſtanch Chief-Maſters of the Woolly
    Woof,
Unſhock'd by Bankruptcies, and Fortune-proof,
Chearily gruff, whoſe Looks of Bus'neſs charm,
Grace in the Front the rugged rapid Swarm.

The Stretch of Rabble, Twelve a-breaſt,
    draws nigh ;
And *(k)* HADDY ! HADDY ! rattles to the Sky.
The honeſt Vogue aſcends Heav'n's ſmiling
    Frame,
Which in approving Ecchoes bids the Name;
And ever, as the duteous Clamours ſoar,
Methinks ſome Angel crys, *Encore ! Encore !*
On t' other hand, from divers Quarters led,
See, growing Squadrons wide FORESTREET
    o'erſpread.

Envy

(k) Haddy.] Mr. Haddy, who had diſcharg'd the Office
of High-Sheriff, and all the inferiour, with Reputation, and
was one of the Candidates at a former Election to the Mayoralty, was expected, and extremely wiſh'd, to have been
again ſet up.

Envy and Emulation ſharp incite
By ang'ring Poſtures to denounce the Fight,
The Mouthy Fight and more.   With mutual
   Grin
They, intricate, to ſkirmiſh ſtrait begin.
Alternate Vollies of adverſe Acclaim
To pierce with miſſive Daunt, bombarding, aim.
A Hundred Throats club Energy of Bawl
For Blue!; a Hundred *for the Yellow!* ſquawl.
O'er the pounch'd Lip Boars foaming Dudgeon
   fumes,
And Dragons Malice hiſſes through the Gums.
Hands clapp'd on Buttocks Fiſts lift braving dare,
And mettled Skips againſt bold Leaps declare.
Brow-beatings glum terrific Frowns oppoſe.
To cope flam'd Cheeks the ſparkling Eye-ball
   glows.
At pointing Fingers levell'd Fingers rage,
And Mouths awry with ſnarling Jaws engage.
High-waving Hats with Hats high-flouriſh'd vie,
Shouts anſwer Shouts, and *Habs!* to *Habs!* reply.
                                                      Vile

Vile Names, like Stinkpots, though to Truth
    unknown,
Are, interchang'd, upon each other thrown:

So is by Wolves afperfive Urine flung,
And the Bonafus battles with his Dung.

In Parts remote the Riffraff, Men and Boys,
With leaning Ears drink the infectious Noife;
And, vainly wifh'd the Field's Remove, to fhare
The hideous Pleafures of the Strife more near,
At once Commotion from each Outfkirt rolls,
And dark Defiles pour out new-mufter'd Sholes.
With trudging Speed their Feet Impatience
    wings,
And, fpringing, to the Camp of Difcord brings:

So, oft', in Bodies, when difpos'd to jar
The Blood impure, and peccant Humours war,
They from th' extremer Parts in Conflux join
Beneath the Arm, or centre in the Groin;

K

Where

Where, bubbling fierce within a Bily Urn, ⎫
Appeafelefs they a new Corruption churn, ⎬
And, wrathful, in vulcanian Tumours burn. ⎭

Bick'ring in Difarray the Pow'rs they find,
Arm'd as with Stings of Hornets in the Mind.
ENTHUSIASM, the hotteft Fiend on Earth,
Hell-born, though it pretends a heav'nly Birth,
Wayward impels the Shock; lewd DISCORD
    leads,
And mad SEDITION bellows at their Heads.

As Dog (I've feen) on Travel, ftung by
    Want,
Arriv'd at Inn, with gnawing Hunger gaunt,
(And by Experience taught a juft Defpair
Of his lefs faithful Mafter's duteous Care)
In Kitchen, cat'ring, fnatch an Offal Feaft,
Or ravin on a Bone, his hard Repaft!
And, bold by Famine, diligent beftir,
Spight of th' inhofpitable menial Cur,

                 Shews

Shews Teeth prepar'd for Teeth, and Yells for
 Howls,
          [Growls,
And renders Snarls for Snarls, and Growls for
So vehement, fo greedy of the Fray,
Rufh the new Comers to th' imbattled Way:
Habs! quick engage with *Habs!* a fkrew'd
 Grimace
Outftares the Gorgon of a wrefted Face;
The rival Buftlers maze a Change of Ground,
And each Side, foaming, thunder *Sound!* for
 Sound!

As, when at Diftance flafhing Sulphurs growl,
And to the Down their grumbled Terrors rowl,
The confcious Shepherd, of experienc'd Ear,
Quakes left the growing Menace burft too near,
The Suburbs round, drain'd of their various Din,
Hear, fhaking, the collected Roar within.

But, fudden Awe! the trembling Streets
 refound,
As though infernal Tempeft fhock'd the Ground!

K 2   And

And fee the Caufe: — Six fmoaking Steeds
   approach,
With lafh'd-up Fury whifking on a Coach: —
How hurricanian fwift !–No fleeter Kind
Are father'd, in the ILIAD, on the WIND.
So glow their working Noftrils, as they run,
As if the fiery Courfers of the SUN
Wedded terreftrial Mares, with proud Defign
To raife a Stud, half mortal, half divine.

Back! back! unfwift of Foot! His Life's at
   ftake
Who dares acrofs the Canal Refuge take:
No more the JEHU would his Gallop ftay
Than (*l*) TULLIA, limp'd his Father in the
   Way.

                       Lefs

(*l*) TULLIA, &c.] Learned and Well-read Perfons need
no Note here; yet for the fake of lefs informed others, 'tis
hoped they'll not abhor one, tho' not of the fhorteft Size.
TARQUIN furnam'd *the proud*, Son-in-law to SERVIUS
TULLIUS, King of *Rome*, inftigated thereto by his execrable Wife, the above TULLIA, confpired againft his faid
Father-in-law, and by Affaffination murther'd him in the
                           Street.

Lefs rapid rattling are Stage-Drivers known,
Of Cattle oftentatious, through a Town.
Upward he threatful Courfe to Hôtel takes,
And all along each lofty Manfion fhakes.

Now 'ftablifh'd Churches fancy Perils more
Than fharp (*m*) SACHEVERAL defcry'd of Yore.
The fundry Gates, Eaft, Weft, North, South,
   and Kay,
Feel joint Concuffion and a joint Difmay:
And fear might Gates which the Chief Temple
   guard,
Left, tumbling, they expofe again the *Yard*,
                   The

Street. And this impious Wretch riding triumphantly in
her Chariot through the fame Street, her Driver, ftruck
with Horrour at the Sight of the bleeding Corpfe, ftopp'd
his Horfes. She call'd to him to go on. He told her, he
could not without driving over her own Father's Body.
She flung a Stool that was in the Chariot at his Head, commanding him to drive on. He obeying, fome of her own
Father's Blood ftuck to her Chariot Wheels, &c.

(*m*) SACHEVERAL.] Dr. HEN. SACHEVERAL, famous at the latter End of Q. ANNE's Reign, for a Sermon,
twice preach'd, on the Danger of the Church, from the
Text *In Perils among falfe Brethren.*

The feparated *Yard,* to Gangs who cou'd
Shed a new worthier (*n*) John the Chaun-
ter's Blood,
Did Chaunters ftill, 'like fuperftitious, creep
To warble Pray'r fo early, half afleep.

Around the Walls a panic Horror fpreads,
And the torn Caftle quick Deftruction dreads:
For fcarce more thund'ring in Egyptian Wars
To Battle rufh'd Scyth-arm'd their Iron Carrs,
As now this defperate (*o*) deck'd Carr of Hides,
Twice twofold Murder rolling on its Sides.

Tremendous Ætna in his Bull-Face glows,
From whofe ftrong Hold the Rein full length-
en'd flows,
Chin, Cheeks, Nofe, Forehead, all of Ruby feem,
And like Carbuncle his flam'd Eyeballs gleam.
Pyrois,

(*n*) John the Chaunter.] A Chaunter of St. Peter's of that Name was heretofore murder'd in the Cloifters,
as he was early in the Morning going to celebrate Mattins.
(*o*) So I venture poetically to ftyle a Coach.

(*p*) Pyrois, fell Planet! in his Orbit ne'er

So fir'd of Afpect roll'd his bloody Sphere.

Nor the Poftillion, in Tann'd Coat of Mail,

And Ox-hide Helmet, fails with Look t' aſſail:

So valiant, keen, and eager to fubdue,

Each darts his Glance — to run a Thoufand
    through.

Horfemen, their Petronels in Holfters plac'd,

With Crefts embofs'd, and gorgeous Cyphers
    grac'd,

A cramm'd flick Troop, in Livery *a-fort*,

Politely ruſtic, the gay Wheels efcort.

October briſkly mantles in the Eye,

And Roaft-Beef Gravy feems the Lips to dye.

Though bulky Beef-Men of the Moon-fac'd
    Guard
                   [ny hard,

Shew Cheeks lefs broad, and Backs lefs braw-

Yet whiſker'd Huſſars, fierce in Caps of Fur,

Lefs briſkly bold to fudden Skirmiſh fpur.

                        Such,

(*p*) Pyrois.] A Name of the Planet *Mars.*

Such, lo! the Equipage. — Shall CLIO tell
What (*q*) Hero loads the vaunting Vehicle ?
No ; — fmiling gravely, fhe refers the Strain
To her fweet Sifter of facetious Vein,
Who thus, — perfifting in the comic Pin,
Sings *What*, — not *Who*, — the mighty MARS
within.

A fhot-free Warrior, who, in Home Cam-
paigns,
　　　　　　　　　　　　　　[Swains;
Commands Dog - Armies, and Dog - kindred
And, train'd a modern NIMROD of the Field,
Makes modern Wild-Beafts -- of the Paddock --
yield,
That not HIRCANIA's Foreft-Records tell
There Tygers by fo vaft a Havock fell
As fall the dreadful'ft Harts, whilft boldeft Hares
Are vanquifh'd eafily as RUSSIA's Bears.

.　　　　　Brave

(*q*) *Heroe.*] This Picture of a Coach and Six, &c. was
drawn from the Life, allowing for poetic Embellifhment.—
[*This Gentleman was fome Honourary- Freeman ; though indeed,
and in ferious and folemn Truth, I have forgot particularly
Who.*]

Bravely as fharp-fet TROJANS, for their Food,

Fought Harpies, he affaults *Cocks* o' the *Wood*:

Undaunted as an *Afric* Hunter tracks

The Oftrich, he fell Patridges attacks;

.And fats a more inhofpitable Way

With Blood of Snipes, — and fuch dire Fowls

 of Prey!

Ev'n HE, for Country's Good, leaves Country

 Chace,

To head fome City Dregs of Populace;

Leaves the fymphonious Howlings of the⎤

 Hound,   ⎬

That Packs of Human Barkers may furround,⎟

And with more favage Harmony cry *Sound!*⎦

 But hufh! For lo! a more than tuneful

  Strain

Enchants the Ear: A long and noble Train,

Approaching, captivates my dazzled Eye,

So bright, fcarce MORN fo brightly gilds the

 Sky.

    L   Say,

Say, whofe the Tweadle-tweadle fweet, who
   thofe
That the long bright Proceffion thus compofe,
In Order, as, with too impeded Speed,
They their fuperior Chiefs-of-Rule precede.

In prime ; a fpruce yet formidable Clan
Come marching, as the Civil Army's Van,
Hight Conftables, well knowing of their Weight,
And Title, once *(r) imperial* of Conceit.
His Step each fortifies with Staff, full quaint
With Deçorations of refulgent Paint :
As TROJANS trufty, *(s)* with a righteous View
Cull'd all to act *impartial——for the Blue.*

                          How

(*r*) *Conftable* being deriv'd from *Koning* - ftable, and from
Koning comes the abbreviated Title *King.*

(*s*) *With a righteous View.*] All the Conftables are of the
Blue Party, as the Party affects to be intitled. Their being
thus cull'd is a notable Inftance of Juftice and Impartiality !
And who can fufpect an ill Caufe to be under-hand ferv'd
thereby, fince Magiftrates of any Honour and Confcience
would deteft and fcorn any vile Management ? To be fure
their candid and neighbourly Defign is only to take the
Trouble of keeping Peace, &c. &c. off the Hands of
others.

How wife, how juft, the Project thus to bar
Againft the Perils of *unnat'ral* War!
For when the wicked God of Faction finds
An equal Pow'r plac'd with repugnant Minds,
In Colleague Breafts he kindles hoftiie Spite,
And goads the very Guards of Peace to fight:
Whilft here's the fole Contention and the Pride,
Who beft can buftle on the *rightful Side.*

But — foftly, Muse : — That Leader ONE
   difplay,
Who ftruts fuch an important *(t)* A per se.

Of bonny Port, a-head the gallant reft,
His tipp'd Battoon now ftay'd an-end on Breaft,
Now in his Grip—(too dignify'd to wield
A Peftle more !) – by the pois'd Middle held,

       L 2   With

(t) A per se.] That is to fay an *A by himfelf* ; the Van-
leader of the Alphabet, the heading Letter, the very *Alpha,*
the Prime of all the fubfequent ones. CHAUCER ufes the
Phrafe, and it is a very fignificant one. I abhor no expref-
five Words for their being *antique.*

With moſt puiſſant Sail their *(u)* choſen Chief
Steers his rigg'd Pageantry of Manly Beef.
What happy Union in his Eye we ſee!
Where Sweetneſs has eſpous'd Ferocity!
Parts in his Frame PARIS and HECTOR crave;
Strong, elegant, briſk, beautiful, and brave.

With leſs Decorum Chriſtmas Mummer ſtruts
Than on He bears his goodly Grace of Guts,
Though that ſame Mummer *(x)* ENGLAND'S
    HEROE plays,
And Dragon with his Whineard's Flouriſh ſlays.

No

(*u*) CYANUS, al. GEORGEF, the Druggiſt, who gat to
be the *Captain Conſtable* by bidding higheſt for the Short Staff,
and procured it to be tipp'd at each End with Silver, his
Name engrav'd thereon, with the Date of the Year. ·
    (*x*) *England's Heroe.*] St. George for *England.* At
Chriſtmas are (or at leaſt very lately were) Fellows wont to
go about from Houſe to Houſe in *Exeter* a *mumming*; one
of whom, in a (borrow'd) Holland Shirt, moſt gorgeouſly
be-ribbon'd, over his Waiſtcoat, &c. flouriſhing a Faulchion,
very valiantly entertains the admiring Spectators thus:
    " Oh! here comes I Saint *George*, a Man of Courage bold,
    " And with my Spear I winn'd three Crowns of Gold.
    " I ſlew the Dragon, and brought him to the Slaughter;
    " And by that very means I married *Sabra*, the beauteous
    " King of *Egypt*'s Daughter, — Play Muſick."

No HAMLET's Ghoft can more majeftic hold
His Truncheon, nor Stage·HANNIBAL fo bold;
Nor one of all the *(y)* Raggamuffian Guard
Of South'nhay Fair more ftately bears the *Yard.*
See! whilft *aright* wide-throated Franticks fhout,
With nodded Thanks he chears the rafcal Rout;
His Ruffle fhak'd encourages the Roar,   [o'er.
And fmil'd Rewards his gracious *Muns* flood

Next *(z)* BEADLES (as in Packs of Cards be
    (a) Knaves,
Two Couple juft) with Brazen-headed Staves,

                               In

(y) Raggamuffian Guard.] A Fair being held in our *Southernhay* Aug. 1. a Parcel of moft be-tatter'd Fellows, furnifh'd with Truncheons, of about a Yard in Length (and therefrom, I fuppofe, denominated Yardf·men) are fworn to keep the Peace, &c. &c. &c.

(z) Beadles.] Thofe whom we commonly call *Stave-bearers*, from the *Staves* with large brazen Heads which they carry in their Hands on Duty. In the Chriftmas Quarter they become Bell-men of the Night, and thump carefully and frightfully at our Doors, at every Turn repeating, in the moft abominable manner that can poffibly be conceiv'd a Bull-dog could by the Gift of Speech pronounce with a Flint-ftone in his Mouth, the moft wretched and hideous Rhymes ever made by the vileft *Devil of a Poet.* See p. 83,

(a) Knaves.] or Gnaves, The Name originally means
                                   no

In tuck'd Blue Vefts, and Bonnets Gold of Brim,

(What Turk's Head Sign ftares, tho' muftach'd,
    fo grim ?

Whofe Brows o'erwhelm'd with *(b)* Varlet
    Haughtinefs

Them fignalize Journeymen-Juftices,

March, throwing Looks of Magiftracy round,

As if to menace Stocks, *Backgate,* or Pound;

(Stocks for th' Unupright, or *poor* Swearer's
    Feet,

And Pound for Hogs caught vagabond in Street;

Where ftarving oft' the Strollers wail, attack'd

By *trading* Juftice on the Vagrant Act).

The Staves they bear, — from whence *Stave-
    bearers* we

Them call, — are Staves of Vaffal Dignity ;

Not thofe which in black Winter Nights with
    Knock

From Reft us ftartle — but to learn the Clock,

                          Or

no worfe than mere *Servants,* (thus in an old Tranflation, *Paul a knave of Jefus Chrift*), or Serjeants, *Servientes.*

   (b) Varlet, perhaps, meant little more formerly than does *Valet* now.

Or feel tremendous Rhyme, in mumbling wife

Croak'd horrible, our tingling Ears chaftife,

When difmal Voice, and difmal Clink of Bell,

Inflict *Good-Morrows* with *(c) Death, Judg-*
ment, Hell.

Minftrels, in Cloaks, for Age how reverend!

From whofe grac'd Necks priz'd Silver Chains
depend,
　　　　　　　　　　　　　　　　　　[blow

Come, whofe Baffoon, Trump, and Recorders

Exftatic Glee before the Grandee Show;

Whilft on each Side a Vocal Thunder peals,

And far and wide the walking Pomp reveals;

Crowds upon Crowds, as in capricious Trance,

As if to ramm the ftarting Pavement dance.

The

(c) Death, &c.] This refpects thefe their Verfes (which
indeed may be efteem'd their beft) viz.

" There is Four Things confider well,
" Death, Judgment, Heaven, and Hell;
" Which if in Caufe you do neglect,
" Unquiet Reft you may expect;
" Good-morrow Mr. *Such an one* (Thump!) &c. &c. &c.

Though I am apt to fear that *if in Caufe* many among us
did *not* neglect to confider of thefe Four Things, they would
take lefs quiet Reft than ufually they *take*.

The trampled Stones refound, and ev'ry Door
And Cafement rattle at the glad Uproar.

So when fweet ORPHEUS ftruck the artful
    Chords,
That eloquently warbled magic Words,
A frifky Joy Bulls, Boars, and Bears poffefs'd,
And Apes and Affes vy'd to caper beft;
Dales, Hills, and Woods, and Rocks, and
    Dens around,
Kept Time in Rapture at the quick'ning Sound.

In gorgeous Robes, and Hats fuperb of Lace,
Four Serjeants follow, each with mighty Mace;
Not thofe dull (*d*) piteous Toys which heretofore
HAIN, OXENBERE, EVANS, and STAPLEHILL
    bore,
                                        Whofe

(d) Toys.] They have now very handfome Maces. But
their former ones were fuch pitiful Things as might deferve
Ridicule almoft as well as the Mace of *Lydford*, defcrib'd
by the old Poet Mr. *Brown* thus,
        ' A Piece of Coral to the Mace,
        ' Which there I faw to ferve in Place, '
        ' Might make a good Child's Whiftle.'
But ours, I confefs, might have been converted into tolerable Punch-Ladles.

Whofe hollow Knobs, and Stems minute and
    fhort,

Shew'd as for Rattles made and Childrens Sport,

But crown'd, and fo magnificent in Mode,

They'd worthily Four Heralds Shoulders load.

    Be-crown'd with Cap of an Umbrella's Size,

Rich Velvet, richer in Embroideries,

Comes burley He, who, as of Spades the King,

Bears Sword erect ;— a fine and fearful Thing.

Cou'd Duke inrob'd at Coronation e'er
                  [bear ?

With Gait more courtly the *(e)* CURTANA

Or cou'd a *(f)* Lictor's Ax and Fafces fpread,

If drawn from its fair Scabbard, keener Dread ?

    Behind this Guardian Armour-bearer pace

The PRÆTOR and his PEERS, Brace after Brace;

Ah! too opprefs'd to ambling fweep along

Through the Ten-deep, clofe-thrufting, noify
    Throng,

           M   Though

(e) Curtana.] The unpointed Sword borne at Coronations.
(f) Lictor's Ax and Fafces.] Such were borne before the
Confuls and Emperors of antient *Rome.*

Though is with Buſtle a ſtreight Alley made,
And pious Bowings own the dread Parade.

Who, and how dignify'd, grave Goodeſs, ſay
The Sages of the Worſhipful Array :
Say, has Lycurgus here aſſum'd the Gown,
And Solon, Side by Side, took Rule in Town ?
Say Muse.   No : — Cautious of Conſtruction
  wrong,
A trembling Veneration checks the Song.
Nor She thoſe Graces hopes to deck her Lays
Which join'd *whilom* in Sir John Adee's Praiſe,
Whence Bays ſo vaſt foreſtalling *(g)* Barret
  won,
He hardly left a Leaf to browſe upon ;
Who Phoebus' Son *thrice* told ! his own Work
  ſung,
                                          [rung ;
Whilſt, hackling ſawn, his Grumbler - Viol

                                          That

(g) *Barret.*] A Fellow who went about with a Baſe-
Viol (though he never could play one Tune in his Life) on
which he, as we may ſay, hack'd and ſaw'd a grumbling
gruff Noiſe, calling it *playing Baſe.* He was the Author of
the Ballad on Mr. Adee, who aſſum'd, in Joke, the Title
of *Sir John Adee.* See more in a ſucceeding Note.

That ne'er fo gruff a Melody cou'd fpring
From a *Morifcan* Bladder-and-a-String.
Time-nicking Bard ! who with fuch cogent Eafe
Could'ft the refined Tafte of CHAMBER pleafe !

Thus the like ruftic lucky Lays could bring
On PAN the laudful Judgment of a *(h)* King.

That *chofen* Band whom we the Vaward faw,
The executive Potence of our Law,
Ent'ring the Roof of Juftice, Strife, and Storm,
With order'd Staffs a Lane, detruding, form ;
Which ere CHIEF-RULERS through can pene-
trate,
[Gate ;
Th' impatient Million jaumbing choak the
And there might ftick, but that th' effective
Sway
Of backing Shovers clears th' obftructed Way.
Rough Anarchy floods blund'ring in amain,
And furly Riot chafes perverfe to reign.

M 2   Routs,

(*h*) *King.*] Viz. MIDAS, who decree'd the Prize to
PAN, even againft the God of Mufick and Poetry himfelf,
APOLLO, or PHOEBUS.

Routs, after Routs, 'fore-ftumbling Routs
difplace,

Then to new Forcers yield the feized Space.

The vaunting Hectors of athletic Frame,

Whom does *Exonian* Speech (*i*) RUMBULLIANS
name,
                                   [fcorn
Cleave with tempeft'ous Drift the Prefs, and

To find a Paffage, fince to make it born.

Like that bold (*k*) Keel which broke ftrong
    VIGO's Boom,
                                   [Room :
The headlong Ruffians burft themfelves a

                                   The

(*i*) *Rumbullians.*] We *Exonians,* who have fome Words
peculiar, I believe, to ourfelves, call furious, headftrong,
headlong, boifterous Men, *Rumbullian Fellows.*

(*k*) *Keel.*] Keel, as poetically does *Carina* in Latin,
heretofore fignify'd a whole Ship. But without having
Recourfe to fuch its old Meaning, or to a *Figure* in
Rhetorick, it is properly enough us'd in its prefent Accep-
tation of only Part of a Ship   The Exploit here referr'd to
is in the Expedition at Vigo, in 1702, when Admiral *Hop-
fon,* in the *Torbay,* cutting his Cables, and clapping on all
his Sails, bore up upon the Boom laid acrofs the Streight,
and broke through it at once ; though it was made up of
Mafts, Yards, Cables, Top-Chains, and Cafks, faften'd
together with Ropes, feveral Yards in Circumference,
under-run with Hauzers and Cables, and kept fteady by
Anchors caft on both Sides of it.

The Numbers, fwagging, on each Flank give
    way ;
For Force muft over-bearing Force obey. .

Thus, mid - way the Canal (*l*), where
    Drudges flow
                           [tow,
To *(m)* Isca's Port Ship, Barque, and Lighter
With maffy Bars Wights of herculean Brood
Sluice-Fenders lift, to equalize the Flood ;
O'er violent the eager Waters gufh
Through the fmall Opes, and onward roaring
    pufh,
Dafh rapid on the ftaky Banks, the Soil
And Pebbles thence expel, high-froathing boil,
And the whirl'd Pond with mad Conteft im-
    broil.

                                But

(l) Canal.] There is a Paffage cut for Ships to and from
Topfham, vulgarly call'd the *Ha'en,* corruptly, or con-
tractedly, for *Haven.* The particular Place here meant is
what we properly enough call the *Double Lock.* The Defcription of the Water's violently gufhing thro' the Sluice,
&c. is precifely natural and juft.

    (m) Ifca's Port.] The Kay of Exeter.

But heark! That Bell which yells a fwift
Alarm
[too warm,
When (*n*) guilty Hearths inflame the Town-
Now, on the Guildhall's lofty Forehead fwings,
And, quick, around its warnful Tinkle flings.
Its Jingles to more clofe Attendance call
Attending Freemen in th' interiour Hall.

Up Stairs direct fair *Ceremony* leads
Sedate to Confult the determin'd HEADS :
For wifts Sufpicion, hank'ring near the Door,
The Confult's but of Things refolv'd before.

But not behoves it our mean MUSE to learn
State Myfteries of fuch a high Concern.
Let her, content, a furer 'Track purfue,
And fing but Matters level with her View.
And what though Tongues of Virulence may
flirt
Their low Afperfions of malignant Dirt,

Short

(*n*) When Chimneys are on fire, this Alarm Bell is rung ;
and the Inhabitant of that Houfe whofe Chimney was in a
Blaze, is to fuffer a Fine.

Short of the Reach are the foul Slanders ſhot,
Scorn'd and derided, nor at all beſpot.

So the firm Guildhall high erects its Head,
And, while Straw-Bonfires choaking Darkneſs
ſpread,
Its briſk Serene's ſcarce fully'd by the Cloud,
Nor dreads the Rage of widen'd Gutter's Flood,
Heedleſs ſees wizzing Squibs and Crackers fly,
And bids the Rocket's direr Bounce Defie.

But worſhipful laſt Year's Triumvirate,
The Leaſh who aid the PRÆTOR's Chair of
State,
Share his Fatigues of Law, nor let, 'tis ſaid,
His Worſhip ev'n at Dinner want their Aid,
But help at taking Bowl as well as Bail,
At *ſtuffing Jerkins* as at ſtuffing Jail,
Call'd STEWARDS now, but *erſt* were BAILIFFS
nam'd,
Ere *Catchpoles* had the honeſt Style defam'd)

In

In fable Robes, which on the Shoulders rife
In folemn fort, and fhape the Afpect wife,
Prefide at Board below, — or haply treat,
Their apt Ambition with the Judgment Seat.

With Warrants ftamp'd on each officious
Face
Staff-Officers, too, feize th' internal Place :
Thick as the Darts which mounts the Porcu-
pine
Their Arms erect with gilded Glory fhine.

Now Walnuts crackle 'tween the Grinder
Jaws,
And bufily engage the peeling Claws ;
While brifk the Glafs, with whittling Sherris
crown'd,
[goes round ;
Quips, Bams, and Bobs, and waggifh Fraud,
Jokes which did ISCA pride in, when *'twas* Wit
To twirl the Hat, twitch Wig, or Knuckles hit;
To tickle with a Straw, or fplafh your Shin,
Diftort the Face, twick Ear, or thruft a Pin.

A

A Monkey fo by Mows and Frifks attefts
Himfelf the Wit moft parluus of the Beafts.
But moft of Wit claims he who greateft Share
Of Nuts can fcrabble, or of Bottle clear.

The chewing Bibbers ftrike with envious
    Pain
The Routs behind, who fuck their Lips in vain,
Unlefs fome noting Friend-in-Court beftow
A Bumper,— or for Kindnefs,—or for Show.

Mean while thofe Courtiers, thus at Banquet,
    loud,
Keep Time fymphonious with the outer Crowd,
Who, burning to the Strife, in Toil rejoice,
Profufe of Sweat, and prodigal of Voice;
And as they more imbibe the hoftile Jar,
They thirft the more infatiate of the War.
Lefs, and lefs furious, fwells the mingled Roar,
When Winds and Billows ftorm at once the
    Shore.

For *Colour* chiefly the Difputes abound,
And Rants for the momentous Beft of Sound.
Some for the *Yellow* hoarfly yell, and fome
Belch grofly *Blue!* — unknowing both for *whom.*

¶ A Moment now again to rooflefs Air,
For more diftinct Infpection, MUSE! repair;
The baleful Fruits of rougher Strife explore,
Or young in Bud, or rotting-ripe at Core.

Around pay'd Eyes fee fervent Rifings glow,
Of Caft more various than the Show'ry-Bow;
And Teints of Or and Azure on the Cheeks,
The *Blue* and *Yellow,* ftriving Hues, commix
A fady *Green,* which *Vert* learn'd Heralds call,
And Gules and Sables, *Red* and *Black,* withal.
See halting Legs fore to the Senfe proclaim
Their Wrench by Wreftlings, or by Spurns
    their Maim.
See, fqualid Patches on the bunch'd Brows tell
What Knuckles have bang'd up a motly Swell.

See

See, clótty Stains, red, dribbled on the Clothes,
Mark Civil Blood ſhed by uncivil Foes,
Whoſe unbroke Buffet, or ill-warded Poach,
The Temples ſcarr'd, or ſet the Noſe abroach.

Survey that Tow'r of Fleſh with ſawcy Pride
Grieving yond' Pillar with his leaning Side,
As if an Ape of SAMPSON bent to move
The Frontier Columns from their Charge above.
What Name ſoe'r might his firſt Sponſors chuſe,
The licens'd Verſe ſhall that of CARNAGE uſe.
Reſerv'd of Voice, compact of Force, he ſtands,
Moroſe & glum, with croſs'd imboſom'd Hands.
His gloomy Looks affect a ſterner Air
Than HOGARTH's (*) hack'd grim Swordſman
      in the Fair,
And, glouting ſcornful, with Defiance watch
For ſome Mob-AJAX, ſole a worthy Match ;
Nor own him yet ; but with diſdainful Toes
He mean-time ſpurns approaching meaner Foes.

N 2   So,

(*) See Southwark Fair by HOGARTH.

So, as the Bull at Stake like grimly ſtands,
And lours a Challenge to the Shamble-Bands,
Stout duels all their brindled Maſtives round,
And caſts them, falling, to imprefs the Ground;
Though Three ally'd ſhot on he'd work to fling,
Beyond the Safeguard of the partial Ring;
Yet fanghlefs Whelps play'd yelping on he'd
    ſcorn
Should feel the Credit of his chaſt'ning Horn;
But, while aloft adult Dogs whirling fly,
He'd foot their defpicable Puppies by.

Oh blind to Fate! thou too prefuming ſtrong!
The deſtin'd Match, amid the inner Throng,
Like arrogant, will foon the Liſts demand,
And meet thy Vaunting with Correction's Hand;
With wringing Gripe Left-hand on Throat ſhall
    fall,
                                [maul.
And th' heavier Right thy quacking Bofom
Hence, hauking ropy Blood, lame, blind, and
    fore,
                                [deplore,
Thy Morrow's Groans ſhall vapour'd Strength
                                And

And in thy wallow'd Bed be Solace vain

That thy Foe, welt'ring, moans an equal Pain,

Or that Time fitter may clear Stage allow,

And HERCULES lefs neuter to thy Vow : —

For anxious Dread fhall rather plague thy Soul,

Left *Bindings-over* more thy Fifts controul;

End of the Fourth Canto.

CANTO V.

ॐॐॐॐॐॐॐॐॐॐॐॐ

CANTO V.

WHether the haughty Defpot of the
 (*a*) *Air*

In ftormy Clouds ftill holds imperial Chair,

Or in infernal Den awaits his Doom,

Referv'd in (*b*) Everlafting Chains of Gloom,

Above our Soaring mounts, or too profound

Lies for the Plummet of our Guefs to found.

To Clerks more vers'd in Lore abftrufe we leave

Full Proofs on either Side—or both—to weave.

Too

(*a*) *The Air.*]   According to EPHES. ii. 2. *The Prince
of the Power of the Air, the Spirit that now worketh in the
Children of Difobedience.*   See alfo Hiftory of the Devil.

(*b*) *Everlafting Chains,* &c.] According to JUDE, ver. 6.
*The Angels which kept not their firft Eftate, but left their
own Habitation, he hath referved in Everlafting Chains
under Darknefs, unto the Judgment of the great Day.*—
II. PETER ii. 4. *Caft them down to Hell, and delivered into
Chains of Darknefs, to be referved unto Judgment.*

Too well we know, though we too rarely mind,

His *(c)* *Angels* here too frank Reception find,

When whifp'ring fly Temptation to the
    Thought,

And twitching by the Paffions to be naught.

(d) Not that, as in *Old-time*, now Midnight
    hears

Fiends roaring wake Folk to neglected Pray'rs.

No longer are their Feet fpy'd *cloven* now,

Nor lampy Eyes more broad than *Saucers* glow.

No maudlin Bibbers, tho' they doubly view,

In *(e)* MARY-ARCHES-LANE, by Glance afkew,

See Coffins op'ning, or White Shrouds to ftalk,

Or Palls and Cloaks in black Proceffion walk.

No flafhing Coaches over BELHILL rove,

As if SALMONEUS mimic Thunder drove;

                       Though

(c) *Angels.*) Read MAT. xxv. 41. REV. fii. 7, 9.
THES. iii. 5, &c.

'*(d)* Note, The feveral terrible Things in this Part of the
Poem detailed were really reported, nay and believed, to
have been feen, felt, heard, and underftood, in *Exeter*.

(e) This Lane is one of the moft common Avenues to
the common Burial-Yard, viz. ST. BARTHOLOMEW's.

Though empty *(f)* Cafks, by Rakes from
   Grocer's Door,
Down tumbled 'rumbling, haply ftartle more.
No *Headlefs-Horfe* neighs ftrolling Wench to
   Bed,
                            [*read.*
Nor drives Boys, late out-ftaying, home — *to*
No Goblins fluggifh Sabbath-breaker roufe
To hurry to the Church,— fure Safety's Houfe.
A Burglar, loaden with new-plunder'd Pelf,
Efpies no mortal Thing *(g)* worfe than himfelf.
The Waits may now, in *(h)* *blackeft Month,*
   go through
Ev'n the *fufpicious* Clofe of BARTHO'MEW,

                                    Nor

(f) At the Head of Bellhill lately lived a Grocer, who
too often left empty Hogfheads all Night at his Door, at
but a narrow Paffage.

   (g) *Worfe, &c.*] Thofe who, on hearing Tales of
Walking Devils, &c. in Exeter, wou'd fignify that they
for their Parts never beheld any fuch, ufe to exprefs themfelves thus: — *I thank God, I've gone all Hours of the Night,*
in many fufpicious Places, and yet never faw any Thing worfe
than myfelf.

   (h) *Blackeft Month.*) They have or had a Notion that in
the *black Month* (as they call it when the Days are at the
fhorteft) the Devils are the moft privileged to roam about,
                                      and

Nor by that Calvary hear difmal Groan
But difmal that from fnuffling Courtal blown,
Nor (*i*) *Southgate's* Porter now lets in a Mifs
At Night's dark Noon whom wou'd he fear to
    kifs.

Ev'n in Church-Porches — (Antient Gran-
    dams told) —
In Winter Nights lewd Mormo's,—horrid bold!
By us Bullbeggars *hight*, were yelling heard,
And dev'lifh Rackets in the facred Yard.
Then (*k*) *Jack-in-Lantern* fooling would miflead
Through Bog and Brake the Sot's benighted
    Tread
      O   Sprights

and play their devilifh Tricks ; whereby the ferenading
Waits, in their nightly Walks, us'd very particularly to be
frighten'd, and to fcamper off. Thofe are call'd *fufpicious*
Places where People had hang'd themfelves, died fuddenly,
&c. Churches, and Church-yards, and empty Houfes, ufe
here to be call'd *fufpicious Places.*

(*i*) I remember it was reported, and believed, that,
during the Porterfhip of Old Mr. Nichols at *S. Gate*,
the Devil in Shape of a fine Gentlewoman us'd to give a
fingle Knock, juft after Twelve o' Clock at Night, and
was let in conftantly by him.

(*k*) *Jack-in-Lantern*, the fame as *Will-with-a-Wifp* ;
the *ignis fatuus.*

Sprights were as frequent in void Houfes then

As were in lonely Lanes grim (*l*) *Gagger-men,*

Then frighted Candles gave, by flaming blue,

The fure Oftent fome Ghoft's Approach to rue ;

Down went the Cards, though Trumps, for
    Satan's Books,

And each beheld a Ghoft— in t'other's Looks.

Then in the Streets dead Scavengers wou'd
    drive .

As nat'ral Wheelbarrows as when alive.

In Meadows then, by Moonfhine, frifky Elves

In Circlets, handing, tripp'd to breathe them-
    felves ;

And· where their petty Toes went featly round,

More florid Pafture dignify'd the Ground :

To Nurfe *a-dream* then wou'd they ftealing
    glide,

And foftly draw her Bantlin from her Side,

And

(*l*) *Gaggermen.*) So we ufed to call Plagiaries, Kidnap-
pers, or Boy-ftealers, from the *Gags* they are reported to
clap in the Childrens Mouths whom they have fpirited
away.

And in its ſtead ſlip a young Fairy Brat,
Thrice taller than themſelves, more groſs,
   and pat
As like as if Twin-Brother born to that.

Then Puck — (or Goodfellow) — from
   Room to Room

Hurl'd Comb, Cowl, Shoe, Trowſers, Beads,
   Ladle, Broom ;

And when wou'd fumbling Beldams Pitcher fill,

Joggling their wither'd Arms the Ale he'd ſpill ;

Nay, oft' o'erturn the Chamber's needful Vaſe,

And with foul Deluge ill-perfume the Place ;

Sometimes long Graſs o'er Paths in Knots he'd
   tie,
                      [fly.
And upwards make Doll Milkmaid's Trotters

But now they're baniſh'd quite, nor big as Eft

One to be laſh'd by (*m*) Demogorgon left.

Not Oberon returns ; nor Mab his Queen

By Cynthia's and by Collin's Eyes is ſeen.

(*m*) *Demogorgon.*)   See Dryden's Fable of *The Flower and the Leaf.*

We not their Footfteps fearch: But when we
view

The Graffy Ringlets fhine of greener Hue,

Conclude we Compoft, for Manuring brought,

With richer Juice the bord'ring Verdure
wrought.
                                    [keep
The Fiends which once did frightful Routings

In Porches, now turn out-fhut Dogs afleep.

Hence the old flaming Sprights prove Glow-
worms now,

And Guttur Glympfes Whitens Heads we know.

Hence Death-watches, which often flew the
Sick,

Are now found Infects of a harmlefs Click.

Hence fkitt'ring Rats are Rats, whofe Squeaks
not fcare

With Fairy Talk the fuckling Nurfe's Ear.

To Manhood hence EXONIAN Mothers bring

Ten Politicans ere one (n) *Chan-ge-ling.*

                                    Hence

(n) *Changeling.*) Many vulgar People here in the Pro-
nunciation of the Word make it confift of Three Syllables,
thus: *Chan-ge-ling.*

Hence *(o)* MAURUS *native Wit* retains; and hence

Shrewd *(p)* MANLIUS preferves his *Infant Senfe.*

Hence qualify'd is Boy-Trick B-̤-GHAM *found*

To mate *(q) His Honour,* and difcourfe his Hound.

Hence H-CK-R, manly wife, though maidly fair,

Hath fav'd his *own,* with Senatorian Air,

To *(r) fecond* each great Motion of the May'r.

If then, ev'n *Fairies* have refign'd their Balls,

Affemblies, Rings, Mafks, Wakes, and Feftivals,

Old ACHERON's *mere Dotards,* furely, wou'd

Bo-peeping, terrify us *to be good.*

What *Tempers* worthy of the Style wou'd gin

Our Hearts by Methods that *deter* from *Sin !*

No; the oft' bilk'd *Enticers,* grown more wife,

Now drefs up *lovely* in chous'd Mortals Eyes,

And

(o) WILL. *(p)* JOHN. *(q) Honour.*] Sir H. *N---hc-tt.*
(r) Second.] This finical and auguft Chamber-man, on
the Mayor's propofing a Matter in Council, is prompt to
be the firft to back him, with his — *Mr. Mayor ! I fecond
that Motion.*

And lure with Calls inchanting as the Air
Of FARINELLI in a Theatre.
Hence, (though with Witch and Sorcerer by Act
Of Senate be cut off each *form'd* Compact)
They with *unwitting* Souls gain snug Abode⎫
And, to misguide us from the (s) Gospel Road, ⎬
Attempt to personate Envoys of G O D.   ⎭

    Some they in *Punk*'s, or *Punch-bowl*'s, Shape
      engage,
In *Pelf*'s Form some, and some of *Equipage*.
Some with *High Post* and *Title* in they draw,
Some to make *Equity* unjust—by *Law*.
No few they urge in Aid of *Truth* to *lie*,
Some to take *Peevishness* for *Piety*.
They others tempt to make Election sure
By formal Mein, stiff Neck, and Cheeks
   demure.
                    [take,
Thick - crowding Shoals into their Nets they
By Acts *immoral* for *Religion*'s fake,

                                 Who

(s) Gospel.] The Etymon is *God's Spell*, or God's Word.

Who *Charity's* Defeſt o'er-pay with *Creeds,*
While *warpleſs Faith* attones for *crooked Deeds.*

Whole Caravans of wou'd-look Saints they
    win,
                    [bour's Sin;
Who ſpare their own, and laſh their Neigh-
Or ſtrive with Pray'r an evil Cauſe to prop,
And thank in Pew for fraudful Gain in Shop.
Some Profligates they trick by ſingle *Hoſte*
To keep from going down, when yielding up
    the Ghoſt:
Some to ken Heav'n for Reprobates fly ope,
Stow'd ſafe in hallow'd Soil with certain Hope.
Some they inſnare Miſ duty to purſue
By chriſt'ning one, and chouſing t'other (*t*) JEW.
Some they teach ſpiteful Kindneſs, who abate
To leſs than *Twopence* on the *Pauper*-Rate,
For Amputation of the Votes of ſuch
As poll'd for FORTY-MEN amiſs too much.

                         In

(*t*) *Jew.*] OTTOLENGHE and GABRIEL TREVES.

In PORTUGAL, the Choler of the Prieſt ⎫
They to impriſon, rack, and burn, aſſiſt, ⎬
And play the Devil in the Name of Chriſt. ⎭

But they *inviſible* bear thus the Prize,

Or maſquerading in a ſpecious Guiſe;

Who would be ſhunn d, were their Complexi-
ons *foot*,
[*Foot*,
Nor hid their *Tails*, *Claws*, *Horns*, and *Cloven*

Or from their Throats blue-flaming Belches
broke,

And Noſtrils ſnorted a ſulphureous Smoke.

Yet, would we imp with pilfer'd Plumes
our Wings,

Like ſome, to ſoar ſublime at *flighty Things*,

We, by *Imagination*, might repair
[Air,
Old *(u)* PANDEMONIUM, or build new in th'

And, ſummon'd, there, in helliſh Pomp convene

Wrath's fiery Demons, and thoſe Fiends of
Spleen,
Which

(u) Pandemonium. See MILTON. Like as PANTHEON
means a full. Aſſembly of the Gods, ſo *Pandemonium* ſigni-
fies that of all the Devils.

Which factious SOLYMA in Siege fo rued,

Self-ruin'd, by inteftine Strife fubdued :

Where (while in State fit Demons of Command,

And thick around the Goblin Commons ftand)

Might His grim Majefty of Sin harangue,

As in *Miltonian* Mode, his Vaffal Gang.

Then might a Poffe of Hell's Rabble ply

Their fmutty Wings, and to EXONIA fly;

And in the Blood of her ferocious Hofts,

The Stygian Legions take their deftin'd Pofts.

But as the MUSE in beaten Tracts to fhine ⎤
Difdains, fhe wou'd *Machinery* decline,   ⎬
Proud to have fprung of no afpiring Line.   ⎦

Nor needs fhe an *exotic* Rage afcribe

To goad a born-and-bred-to Fury Tribe,

Whom if to line fuch *hellifh Mobbers* ftrove,

They might themfelves in *Belial Acts* improve.

Suffice it, then, to fay, their Earthly Kin

Chafe as if did *a Legion* fume within :

P   Their

Their own ERYNNIS. to the MUSE confeſt,

More fires the Brain, more ſtimulates the Breaſt.

For we already have digreſs'd too long,

And ought reſume the interrupted Song.

MUSE ! teach me Notes adapted to rehearſe

Strife rais'd to Tempeſt in congruent Verſe !

And ſafely ſuch bold Hurricane to form,

Curb THOU its Fury, and control the Storm ;

Yet whatſoever Pitch the Numbers fly,

Let ſmiling HUMOUR ſtill accompany.

Count it the Inſtant when NED's Face o'Fire

To five Hours Cooling leaves the heated Quire,

And, with a *Back - Lane* Cogue 'new-fuel'd,
glows

                 [*Roſe* ;

Through EASTGATE, redder then an *Auſtr'an*

Then, turn'd from LONDON-INN tow'ds LI-
VERY-DOLE,

Makes PARIS-STREET to dread a flaming Coal,

                             That

Five Hours, &c.] That is between Prayer and Prayer
Time, from Eleven till Four.

That each poor Dweller, anxious, eyes his
    Thatch,
                            [hatch.
Left reaching Sparks *(z)* new Conflagrations

Mean-while Throat-Battle rages; Party Cant
Mingles its foul Antiphone of Rant:
The Babel Clamours, varying, around;
Thus plainly, with confus'd Diſtinction, found:
' *Blue !*--Yellow !-- Sound for HADDY!-- *Sound*
    for HEATH !
                       [*to Death !*
' *H-a-b ! Sb--ſack !*—Sound for Yellow—*Blue*
' *The Church for ever !* — Down with PERKIN's
    Crew !
                       [*for Blue !*
No Courtiers ! — No Mock Patr'ots ! — *Sound*
And not a Mouth but what, expanded large,
Does thrice a Threeſcore Times its Load diſ-
    charge ;
And *Rogue !* and *Dog !* and *Raſcal !* and *You lie !*
At ev'ry Turn aſſiſt the ſtriving Cry.

Dreadful

(z) New Conflagrations] Great Part of Paris-ſtret having ſome Years ſince been on fire on both Sides the Way,
and the Houſes being, nearly all, Thatched.

Dreadful Ado ! Ere clafh'd encounter'd Swords
To match fuch combating Hodgepodge of
  Words ?
Were in *Old* Chaos the like Garboils found,
Or Jargon Brunts of fo embattled Sound?

  Scarce more fonorous in their turbid Cave
Heard MARO's MUSE contending Tempefts
  rave.

  Like waving Reeds, when Gufts in Auguft vex,
Near lowmoft Sluice, the oozy Fens of EXE,
The brabbling Multitude, amid their Cry,
Flag where o'erwhelm'd, and with the Tide
  comply.
If were an antick World of Franticks pent,
To dance the hay, in wild Vagary, bent,
Scarce could the reftlefs Bedlams, winding, pace
Such tangled odd Viciffitude of Place :
Nor were they chang'd in Brain to Wolves,
  they'd grin
To bark fo harfh, fo horrible, a Din.

'Tis

'Tis Blifs, they deem, diftracting tofs'd, to rowl;
And fouleft Pudder recreates their Soul.

So when rough Æolus's bluft'ring Train
To foamy Mountains blow the Fluid Plain,
Tumult'ous *(a) Fifh - Hogs* tumbling Tricks
    perform,
Aid the Waves Uproar, and enjoy the Storm.

Scarce ever Sheriff's Subftitute cou'd fee
Such rampant Bick'rings fhake our *Heavy-Tree,*
Where, with authoritative Pikes of Afh,
Bailiffs the Head-defending Cudgels thrafh.
Ne'er did fuch petulant Confufion rage,
In Weftgate-Quarter on *(b)* Whit-Monday's
    Stage ;
Where bumping Thwacks and the Wail-rai-
    fing Drub
With vaunted Glory Blockhead-Heroes dub,
                    Till

(*a*) The Porpoifes, or Porcu-pifces.
(*b*) Every *Whit-Monday* tnere is in this Place erected
a Stage for Cudgel playing, &c. round about which, as
well as on it, are ufually moft terrible Doings.

Till Pates, fad Turn of War! in dripping Flood,
Afham'd, give forth the honourable Blood.
Scarce feels our Clime more of Perdition full
At a *(c) Prætorian* Beating of the Bull,
When Their fage Worfhips the Town-Pails
    allow
                        [throw.
Colds, Fevers, Deaths, in chilling Streams, to

  Elbows on Chefts repay from Elbows Grief,
And ftamp'd-on Feet by trampling feek Relief.
Eyes, by flapp'd Hat, with briny Rheum ftruck
    blind,
By like Infliction try a Cure to find.
Bums butting ftickle; Hips, and dafhing Knees,
And rubbing Ankles, fore delighted, teaze.

                        Perukes,

(c) Prætorian Bull-baiting.] About Three Weeks after
the Election of a new Mayor, a Bull ufes to be brought and
baited before his Door: At which Time the moft fcandalous
Abufes are practifed with Impunity, yea Applaufe, by ruffian Butchers, &c. throwing Water, dipt up from the very
Kennel, &c. on all Perfons they can meet with, even in their
own Houfes. The Leathern City-Buckets, prepared for ex-
tinguifhing Fires, are lent to them from the very Guildhall for the vile Purpofe. Rare Doings at Bath! ----- [*The
throwing of Water has been for fome Years difus'd.* 1770.]

'Perukes, now timely made the Pocket's Care,

Leave, apter to throw Knock, ſhav'd Sconces
 bare.

Nor ſtays expos'd (what Place of Wig ſuppl,·)

The worſted Cap, diſtinct with curious Dyes,

Though (*c*) IRIS dipp'd the Woof not, clam-
 my wet,

And ſhining with the Pate's hot Spring of Sweat.

From off the Neck's hawl'd Handkerchief, or
 Stock,

To ſave from Throttle by a coll'ring Shock.

The Shirt diſbutton'd ſpreads its Boſom wide,

Or Sham,— worn clean — no cleaneſt Shirt to
 hide ;
 [defend,
Yet Gripes, ev'n where broad Shoulder-ſtays

Shall hideous Chaſms in ſtouteſt Dowlaſs rend.

Nor Veſt of Drugget moſt robuſt ſhall ſcape,

Nor Coat of Iron Kerſey, though with Cape

Enormous fortify'd, a ghaſtly Width to gape.

Woe

· (*c*) *Iris.*) Alluding to MILTON's " Iris dipp'd the
Woof. "

Woe were the Spot, where,-- chewing Cūds
    of Spite,
                    [Smite.
Fell Champions, met, renew'd the Knuckle-

There GIBBONS, bulky BOLT, tough TAN-
    NER, FRY,

FOOT, HOOPER, ASHLEY, TWIGGS, might
    boxing die,

And cryſtal ISCA reek,— a ruby Flood !

And more than the (*d*) ADONIS run with Blood,

If ſworn Authority, alert at hand,

Staff interpoſe not, and the Peace *command !*

Yet, maugre all --- piqued Braves in fluſter'd
    State,

Prick'd jealous on by Luſt of Fame, or Hate,

And, prompted each by his fomenting Clan,

Strain brutal Force to prove the Better Man.

                            For

(*d*) *Adonis.*] A remarkable River, near *Byblos* in *Phœni-*
cia, at certain Seaſons, and on ſome Occaſions, appears
as if bloody, ſuppos'd (ſays MILTON) with the Blood of
THAMMUZ, yearly wounded. But the ſaid Phœnomenon
was long ago declared to be occaſion'd by a kind of *Minium*
cr *Red Earth,* which the River brought away, when ſwell'd
to unuſual Heights.

For DAREMAN--(óf more overweening Pride
Than (e) GATH's Huge Knight, who ISRA'L's
   Hoft defy'd;
Than whofe none of the pictur'd CÆSARS e'er
Such Jolt-Head did, or Eyes more ftaring, bear;
Firm-fet, and not of Stature high; full grim
His rough-hewn Afpect; of ftupendous Limb,
And Flefh all callous)-- DAREMAN thus aloud
Provokes to Single-Loggerhead the Crowd:

  ' Produce a *Man*, ye Scolders of the *Blue*,
  ' If *Men* wou'd harbour with your beftial Crew,
  ' With Me in *Manhood* Skill and Force to try,
  ' While ftand both Armies join'd Spectators by !
  ' And learn ye all from the Event how far
  ' Ye may hereafter venture folid War:
                         [Boys,
  ' Bold though ye dare, by Females help'd and
  ' To form Attack with Blufterings and Noife:
  ' His Groans repentant fhall foon caufe to know,
  ' Tis ours to vanquifh with effective Blow.'

         Q   He

(e) Gath's Knight.] GOLIAH of *Gath*, a Giant.

He faid, clench'd hard his maffy Fift, and ftruck
Ten mighty Wherrets with one fighting Look.

Promifc'ous Clamours differently rife,
Some to explode, fome to carefs and praife:
But " Sound for HADDY !" and fcarce check'd
    Huzzahs!
So loud prevail from the proud *Yellows* Jaws,
That louring *Blues*, abafh'd, a while keep in
Their *(f)* Stink-Word, and fcarce dare a *Hab!*
    to grin.
But fo not long: For murmur'd Talk around
The irritating Challenger refound:
" Thus has the braving Bully done, thus fpoke :·
" What! no Man dare rebuke him with a
    Stroke?
" No Match within ?—Fly, fly, and bruit afar
" Th' Affront among the doughtier Chiefs of
    War."
But FAME, induftr'ous with her Trump, before
More fleetly the diffufive Tidings bore,

                                    And

(f) Viz. Sh-tfack.

And (*g*) ATE, in LONG-PHILL's diffembled
Form,

In CARNAGE blew of burning Ire a Storm:

" Hafte, Thou Dependance of our grateful
Hoft,

" And teach the faucy *Yellows* how to boaft:

" But DAREMAN, if unactive here thou ftay,

" From thee conveys the ufeful Dread away.

" Break thund'ring in.— See ! where the Brag-
gard ftands,

" And proudly brandifhes provoking Hands,

" With Purpofe thee of Glory to beguile,

" And brand thee with a Coward Lubber's
" Style."

(*h*) SHE fpoke, and clapp'd his Loins.   Her
coaxing Breath

Infpires a Vow,—*Within an Inch of Death*

Q 2   To

(*g*) ATE]. The Devil of a Goddefs, viz. of Rage, Difcord, Revenge, Havock, &c. — [*Now in* 1770 *I have*
really forgot the Bullies Names which Long-Phill and Carnage
ftood for.]

(*h*) *She.*] That is, ATE in the Difguife of LONG-
PHILL.

To facrifice to Great Revenge, on Foes,
Whole Hecatombs of Bofom-bafting Blows.
At once a fudden Clap of dreadful Roar
Burfts expeditious through the Archy Door;
For, compafs'd with a Rout of Boutefeus,
A Rout of ruggedeft deep-voiced Blues,
And ftripping as he comes, the bulky Wight
Tow'rs, oftentatious of his Shoulders Height,
The wifh'd Occafion feizing.   Flam'd his Eyes
At once fight, conquer, triumph, tyrannife.
SAMPSON is fung *(i)* lefs confident in Wrath
Addrefs'd to pommel HARAPHA of GATH.

> As when Two warring Ships crowd fail to
>   wage
> A marine Duel, with proportion'd Rage,
> Broadfides exchang'd their furly Greetings throw,
> Ere grappled they their boarding Prowefs fhow,
> So thefe, reciprocal, their Vollies dire
> Of Malediction, ere the Clofure, fire,

And

(i) It fung, viz. In MILTON's *Sampfon Agoniftes.*

And with a belch'd-out miffile Fury warm
Defiance to defy, and Arm meet Arm.
Where, where's the Scoundrel? eager CARNAGE
cries.
                                      [replies.
" Here, Rafcal, here, mov'd DAREMAN bold
I'll rafcal Thee, thou Dog! rejoin'd the firft,
" Villain, come on," the laft adds, and be curft.
Choler no farther Parle allows ; and Space
For Action made would longer Parle difgrace.
But, fhooting prone both with collected Might,
Their obvious Bulks commence fubftantial Fight:
Each Lefthand's Clutches tugging grafp a Foe,
And Righthands clos'd redouble Blow for Blow.

So when grim MULCIBER, for JOVE his Sire,
Laborious forg'd the forky Bolts of Fire,
Tenacious one the wizzing Steel did guide,
The ftronger Arm the pond'rous Hammer ply'd.

The clubby Fifts on Teeth & Trunk refound,
And feem the Brawn with mortal Thumps to
pound.
                                      Chefts

Chefts bruifen jarr, the Ribs as fhatter'd crafh,

And bleeding Jawbones clatter, every Dafh.

Each like *(k)* EPEUS aims deftructive Pains,

And firm as an EURYOLUS fuftains.

Both as *(l)* ENTELLUS Bang with Bang requite,

And hard as DARES bear the falling Weight.

Head againft Head their ftunning Efforts knock,

Like Rams at Duel for the Female Flock ;

Nor Arm will more Neck at Advantage fpare

Than would a HOCKLEY's Maftiff-hugging Bear.

But Legs in-lock'd Antagonift to throw

Oblige that hard Advantage to forego.

The Head retriev'd, loft Moments to redeem

Of fham'd Inaction, wafh'd by Nofe a-ftream,

Leaps up elaftic, and Reprifal draws

Of fcurvy Blood leak'd from the loofen'd Jaws.

Surrounding

(k) EPEUS *and* EURYOLUS.] Names of Two ftout Combatants at the Funeral Games for PATROCLUS in HOMER's Iliad. 23.

(l) ENTELLUS *and* DARES.] The Two Champions at the Games in honourary Memory of ANCHISES in VIRG. Æneid. 5.

Surrounding Routs exclaim more. Space to
　.clear,
And wheel, a living Amphitheatre,
Whilft fome behind the circling Tumult fpring
By Fits to overlook the buftling Ring.
By Wagers fome their Wifhes would fupport;
Some gnarr to fright, and Courage fome exhort;
And partial Sidings to moleft or aid,
Which multiply the Combat, are affay'd.

Soon fpurting Noftrils wou'd dye red the Floor
With Inundations, mixt, of factious Gore,
If ftill remifs of fwagg'ring Duty lay
The Sons of (*m*) THEMIS of fubaltern Sway;
Or niggard prov'd of Breath and fwelter'd
　Greafe,
In troublous Domineering for the Peace.
But foon their Highneffes, whofe huffie Lift
Can, arbitrary, bid the World *affift*,

　　　　　　　　　　　　　　Al!arm'd

(*m*) THEMIS]. The Goddefs of Juftice. Thefe her
Underling Sons mean the Conftables.

Alarm'd at fuch bold Neighbourhood of War,

With ftretching Necks up ftart within the Bar;

When thus *(n)* CYANUS, by officious Words

To fire his Troop to Action, Speech affords :—

" Compeers in Poft! — Do thus our Palms
    " retain

" Thefe dread Infignia of our high Domain,

" Staffs of Controul, which legally fetch down

" All who not own in *Proxy U S* the Crown?

" And in the Prefence, in Our very Court,

" Shall *Sh--facks* of Infurgency make fport?

" I fay,— Before Us, *U S*, whofe awful Word

" MARS ought obey, and drop his lifted Sword,

" (MARS, *in the Garb of fconcing Grenadier,*

" *Who'd (o) Tall rank'd with Tall* PRUSSIA
    Guards appear)

". His

(*n*) GEORGE COMINGS. See before, page   . The
Cyanus properly is the Flower call'd the *blue Corn-bottle*, and
which our Country People name *Pretty-Johns*.

(*o*) The King of Pruffia's Delight in very tall Men for
his Body Guard is not unknown.—[*The late King, Father
of the prefent, is meant.* 1770.]

" His Sword, though for a captiv'd Trull
  'ydrawn,

" Or to retake Habiliments from Pawn;

" Shall Slaves of Orange Badge, fo het'rodox!

" With ours thus interchange pugnacious
  Knocks;

" Nor W E, on whom dares rife no *batt'ring*
  Joint,

" Or ev'n a Finger rear *affaulting* Point,

" Fall in, chaftizing, and Big-ton'd declare,

" With Magifterial Vifage, WHO WE ARE?

" Go to, then; let our brandifh'd Arms
  maintain

" US not *felect* to bear thofe Arms in vain."

He faid. His Mates of Dignity unite

To fpring upon the *tuftling* Crowd in Fight,

Together huddling, fome from off the Bench,

Each with imperious Standard in his Clench,

And back by their arrefted Collars hawl

The Outer Orbits, as for bailefs Thrall;

R   And

And with fierce Features, in a Thunder's Tone,
Cry, " Keep the Peace ! WE reprefent the
    Throne.

Their dreadful Charge the inmoft Circles hear,
Refign the Battle, and to Paffage clear:
For *JOVE* lends oft' to LAW terrific Grace,
And fhakes his Ægis in a Rebel Face.

The Duelifts (though Pride difowns *Enough*,
Howe'er bray'd Jelly, of the martial Cuff)
Permit to break their pertinacious Fangs,
And *fuffer* Shelter 'mid their friendly Gangs.

So (*p*) when the Trojans, forward in the
    Strife
                                   [Life,
For claim'd Patroclus, fpoil'd of Arms and
Heard, from the Rampart by Pelides trod,
Tremendous as of fome deftroying God,
His ireful Call, the Valiant felt Difmay,
And even Priam's braveft Sons gave way.

                                      Our

(*p*) *When the Trojans.*) See Hom. Il. lib. 18.

Our fever'd Heroes, fmear'd with Muck and
Gore,

Baulk'd Anger folace with Revenge in Store;

And, lugg'd indignant each a diverfe Way,—

Drink,--hauk,--drink,--fwear,--drink,--brag a
future Fray;

From the fwoln Face half wipe the bloody Dirt,

And Breeches repoffefs with Tails of Shirt.

Difafters fad one guilty Wretch betide,

Who dar'd, un-franchis'd, join the Yellow Side,

And, that he might the bafting Fifts efchew

Of an 'oer-matching and revengeful Blue,

Had from the ope Piazza of the Hall

Slunk in, where to repeat illegal Bawl:

For, there detected foon, he's clafp'd by Throat,

And charg'd with lawlefs bold Intent to *vote*;

And, with his Shirt, Skin, Hair, & Jerkin ragg'd,

Is to (*q*) the temporary *Baftille* dragg'd.

Somewhat

(*q*) *Temporary Baftille.*) What is call'd the *Back-Gate*, to
which the Conftables arbitrarily, of their own Authority,
commit, by Night, or for a while.

* CERES, the Solace and Support of Life,

Invigorates with ftronger Voice the Strife ;

DEVON's (*b*) POMONA helps the Verbal Broil,

Or cooper'd (*c*) BACCHUS haps to reinforce the
    Coil.

Now Entries flow hot with a Urine Sea ;

And rattling Walls think Water-Engins play,

From whofe ftain'd Corners divers froathy Rills

Shape Courfe in reeking Conflux o'er the Hills ;

In fuch quick Torrents the rank Streams com-
    bine,
                                            [Brine.
That EXE grows warm and brackifh with the

And if well-ftation'd Millmen frugal were,

They their embarrel'd Stock of *Seg* might fpare.

Eels haply think the Tide does downward
  ˌ drive,

And feafon'd Trouts fear pickling while alive ;

                                            Seiz'd

into *Malt,* as well as for brewing afterwards. So *Pomona*
is put for *Cyder,* and *Bacchus* for *Wine.*

(*) *Ceres.*] The Goddefs of Corn and Tillage She is
by a *Metonymy* us'd frequently in Poetry for Wheat, Barley,
Bread, &c.

Seiz'd with Vertigo may the fuddled Dace
Be feen to ramble on the River's Face;
Not with intoxicating Berries dos'd,
But ftronger Fumes fwift from the P--fing-Poft.

Libation made to DISCORD, and renew'd ⎤
Spent Vigour,—they again, at Hall, intrude ⎬
With rallied Hubbub, and reftore the Feud. ⎦
As fiery Bulldogs, when their Shamble-Lords
Slip from their urgent Necks reftraining Cords,
Whofe well-prov'd Holders drip a foamy Gore,
Spring furious at the Bull, tho' tam'd before,---
So fiercely eager the chear'd Party bound,
Ope-mouth'd, more inftant for the Conq'ring
    Sound.   [*moiften'd* Foe:
Juft Dread ftrikes Silence through th' *Un-*
The roaring *Half-drunk* with new Valour glow.
Difhearted thofe fhrink to the Left and Right;
Thefe, glory'ng, in the Centre brave the Fight.

Yet Courage foon reanimates the Fray,
For timely Aid huzzahs not far away,
                     Then

Then breaks all-hideous on the vauntful Crew,

And for the Conqueſt warms the vanquiſh'd few.

Leſs Rage the Myrmidons, on Ilion's Plain,

To ſave the Navy, and avenge the Slain,

Urg'd—than impels the Succours to the Brawl:

Nor flinch the Hardy of the adverſe Squawl.

Not with ſuperior Fury is purſued

A Dog in Paſſage near a feather'd Brood,

When with up-briſtled Plumes, and Quills a-
ſpread,

The ſcolding Hen, ope-bill'd, aſſerts the Shed,

Than what tranſports th' Aſſailants to the
Charge :

Nor, grinning ſurly, with Jaws open large,

The Growler on the plumed Heroin turns

Like Ire as which each grim Defendant burns.

Dire the reviv'd Conteſt : The equal Routs

Pelmell aim Havock with contending Shouts.

Shoves repel Shoves, Breaſt - Bulkings meet
Rebuff ;

But woe the Shins not tann'd to Kicking-proof!

Yet

Yet what *terrene* fhall firm exift *for ay* ?
Lungs tho' of Brafs were fubject to Decay :
Snorts of gigantic Noftrils muft, *at length*,
Own, in fhort Pantings, a Decline of Strength.
Too long, too high, the human Organs fprain'd
Crack, — as in th' Adage Bow too much con-
    ftrain'd.
But though, *at length*, maim'd Voices barely
    croak,
                 [provoke,
And ev'n craz'd Murmurs ftrangling Coughs
Yet fault'ring Grumbles mutter harfh the Cry,
And widen'd Mouths mutely a Roar imply :
Refolv'd, in *laft Refort*, to win Regard,
Like Cocks, and Villains hang'd, by *dying hard*.

    So, at old CHEVY,— (*an old Bardling tells* ;
Though fmil'd at by our modern Infidels)—
When lopping Sword, by nether Chop, has won
The Pedeftals of ftrenuous WITHRINGTON,
Though Lofs of Blood his lower Stroke im-⎫
    pairs,   [rears,⎪
On Stumps,—*the beft he may*,—he Faulchion⎬
And, to laft Gafp, defcending Backfword⎪
    dares.   ⎭

    End of the Fifth Canto.

    S   CANTO VI.

CANTO VI.

THE Vocal Ammunition fpent, *within,*
 A while, furbated, flinch'd the Rage of
 Din ;
And but thin Parties, mazy, here and there,
Without, light fkirmifhing with *Habs !* pickeer:
Tho' *Quill*'s deny'd, yet *bought* Refection drains
Parch'd Legions, panting, from the hot Cam-
 paigns;
And though mixt Numbers ftand oppos'd their
 Ground,
          [wound ;
Battle, ftruck hoarfe, ftrives but with Lours to
Or, folitary, a rare random Cry,
Feebly affay'd, pops difregarded by.

But renovated *Coil* not long allows
A mute Engagement of but hoftile Brows;
For Hoftels divers, near adjacent, yield
Late Invalids, recover'd, to the Field ;
          With

With Effence arm'd of quick-reftoring Mault,
More ftimulated to re-join Affault,
And,--like fell Hounds from 'Fault reclaim'd,--
    more ftrong
To *open,* as they rudely pufh along.

Now, rallying the fcatter'd Routs of *Blue,*
Full by the Sconfe fuperior to the View,
Ample his hairy Cheft, VENTOSO ftands,
A ftern Colofs, and waves his horny Hands,
Demanding momentary Paufe ; and,—large
Expanding Jaws,—refufcitates the Charge:
Ardor full-fcarlet kindles in his Face,
Which, like a Comet, fhoots a threat'ning Blaze;
And thus, with well - ale'd Voice, prepar'd to
    twang
Rafh Defamation, — belches hoarfe Harangue:

    " How ! Yield the Day ? Oh Shame ! oh
      new Difgrace !   [Race ?
" WE, -- WE -- the Day, -- and to the Canter
" Who aim fchifmatically to trapan
" Our *Catechife* with their *Chief-End-o-Man :*

" A fqueamiſh Crew, who'll tremble if We
  ſwear;

" But—in *Damn'd-Lying* take a tenfold Share:

" The Calf's-Head-feaſted Villains, who deride

" Our *Curſe* as *cauſeleſs* on the Martyr's Tide:

" Who wou'd again our Church to *Stable* turn,

" And *juſt-made* Surplices to Tinder burn,

" As but *old* Smocks of BABYLON's old
    Whore;
                                [Pow'r;
" Beat down the *Teſt*, and climb again to

" Who at our nodding Creſts of Oak-boughs
    ſneer,

" And white Roſe from our very Boſoms tear:

" What! ſhall We, daſtardiz'd to Silence, ſeem

" To give the Victory of Voice to them?

" Again that malapert Sleeve-laughing Crew

" In Mourning hang our (*a*) MAUD'LEN daub'd
    with Blue?
                                " Which,

(*a*) *Maudlen*, &c.) *Maudlen*, or properly *Magdalen*,
Gallows, the Execution Tree for High Treaſon, Felonies,
&c. committed within the County or City of *Exeter*.
Divers ſuper-eminent Perſonages of the *Blue* Army (among
whom a Blindman was one) having had the Whim to paint
                                their

" Which,—blaſt their *Peepers!*—might urge to
deſtroy

" In Flames of black *November*'s Fifth their Joy;

" And from ſack'd Conventicles, — but — for
Law ! —

[*(b)* Baxter draw !

" Pews, Canting - Tubs, and Books of

" I ſay, my Bloods ! ſhall of th' *Old Rump* the
Seed

[recede ?

" Think we will *ere* from Cuſtom's Right

" No : Sooner let the guilty *(c)* Sun be gay

" Upon the Royal Martyr's ſacred Day !

" No, my brave Bullies, with rough Shocks of
Breath

" Firſt tempeſt their fanatic Souls to death :

" Your

their Houſes, ſignificantly, of that Colour, to ſhew their
Extravagance of Zeal ;—it happened that, on their loſing
an Election, ſome concealed Wags of the contrary Party
daub'd this Gallows partly of that Colour, and withal hung
ragged *black* Crape upon it, for Mourning.

(*b*) *Baxter's Books.*) James's Meeting-Houſe is, or I well
know was, furniſhed with Baxter's Works, in ſeveral
Volumes, Folio.

(*c*) *Sun be gay.*) I have heard it confidently averr'd in
Exeter, that the Sun never ſhines clear on the 30th of
January. But they err'd egregiouſly, eſpecially while the
Old Style continued among us.

" Your Bellows of diſtended Lungs prepare

" To blaſt the Pimps with ruthfulleſt Deſpair :

" Enforce your Sinews; cloſe in firm Array ;

" And plunge, o'er-turning, in the Depth of Fray."

He ſpoke ; and, ending, thrice with wilful Fiſt
Beat up new-levy'd Anger to aſſiſt.
Th' Imperial Beaſt with Tail's Rib-laſhing Strokes
His Choler thus to boiling Height provokes.

The *Azure Forces* huddling cloſe around,
Feel the Oration's Charm, and club a Sound ;
A Sound ? —Not (*d*) MARS ſo loudly *roaring* ſtood,
When DIOMED had drawn his rabid Blood :
In Vollies rais'd, loud, louder, and more loud,
Tempeſt'ous Onſets vex th' invaded Crowd.
The Orbs of Sight with flaſhing Outrage burn,
While Buſtlings work Confuſion's dire Return.

But --

(*d*) *Mars,* &c.) See Hom. Il. lib. v.

But-- ftorms the Onfet unrepell'd ? Oh ! can

Stand paffive the infulted *Yellow Clan ?* —

As foon could frifky Dancing-Mafters be

Of folid Head, and fit from Fidging free.

As foon could Smiths their Trough's black
    Puddle *fwig*,

And Tuckers fuddle on their flimy *Sig.*

As foon Shoemakers, in a Shilling rich,

Could in a Garret on a Monday ftitch.

As foon could *(e)* CLACK, who all Things
    knows and more,

Whofe Lip with Arts and Eloquence runs o'er,

His Tongue's perpetual Motion ftop, and hear

His Mug-Mates take of Talk fome little Share.

No :—Wroth BENANAK, bulky, tall, in Word

And Act robuft, with dauntlefs *Stingo* fpurr'd,

A forward Chief, of envy'd Fame among

The high-fam'd Mighty of the *Saffron'd Throng*,

Mouths thus,—by Stretch of eager Tone to fire

His touchy Cohorts with intenfer Ire :—

                " League

(e) CLACK.) There's a numerous Race of thofe *Clacks*,
I inftance them in the general Family.

" League of the *Orange* hear ! Brave *Yellow-*
Boys,
                                        [enjoys,
" Whofe *Hue* the Sov'reign Mettal GOLD

" And *Guineas* boaſt the *(f) Name :* Shall
beſtial Force

" Of *(g)* Hogſty Savages uncheck'd ha' Courſe;

" Who're rather like foul Swine themfelves ſo
much,
                                        [touch !
" Scarce naſt'eſt JEW *(h)* the filthy Herd would

" Shall Miſcr'ants, bred in Greaſe, Blood, Draff,
and Dung,   .
                                        [Tongue ?
" Like Vixen Scolds brave *Men* to Tilt of

                                        " Shall

(f) Name.) Viz. of *Yellow-Boys.*

(g) Hogſty Savages, &c.] The Hog-ferving Slaves of the
Shambles. ☞ *N. B.* ' A Hog was heretofore hieroglyphi-
' cally pictured to expreſs an Enemy to Good-Manners,
' and a prophane Perſon.   For the Eaſtern Nations did ſo
' hate a Hog for his filthy Difpofition, that it was a Crime
' for ſome of their Prieſts to *touch* it.'   We make our BEN-
ANAK (or Son of ANAK) exclaim principally againſt thoſe
Enemies to Good-Manners, feeing many of them are
---[i. e. *about the Time of writing were*]--- the Ringleaders,
Strength, and Pride of the Party.   .

(h) Filthy Herd.) Our Journeymen Butchers are ---[i. e.
they at the Date of the Poem were]--- probably, in the general, the moſt beaſtly filthy Fellows, of the Profeſſion, in
the Univerfe. Scavengers and Ridders of Bog-Pits appear
not ſo nauſeous. [*How they are now,* 1770. *I know not.*]

" Shall fuch as from wild BOGLAND's (*i*) Rapparees

" Denomination take,—as beft agrees,—

" Whofe ugly *Hawing* to our Teeth denotes

" Their Prologue to th' old Play of *Cutting*
Throats;
[of ROME,
" Shall fuch mere Mongrels, the Half-fpawn

· " Againft *Whole Proteftants* refiftlefs come?

" Shall Caitiffs whoop, as 'twere for RebelWar,

" Like Varlet Clans led on by Traytor MAR ?

" No, Liegemen, no:— The *Perkinites* fhall
know
[more flow.
" Our Strength keeps firmer, as it moves

" Old Prophecies, I 've heard, in Terms de-
clare,
[Hair.
" The TURK fhall fall by Men of (*k*) *Yellow*

" And fhan't our chriftian *Yellow* Knots fubdue

" The more than heathenifh Cockades of *Blue?*

T   " They

(*i*) *Rapparees.*) A Tory or a Rapparee originally means
the fame Perfon.

(*k*) *Yellow Hair.*) See BAYLE's Dict. Art. MAHOMET,
Note [99].

" They fhall : I fee how they inglorious droop

" Ev'n on the Cockfcombs of their *(l)* Liv'ry
    Troop;

" They fhall :—I fee already how they hang

" Lithe on the Numfkulls of the beggar'd Gang,

" As if from that Old tawdry *(m)* Vefture torn

" By Madam Blowza's foggy Buttocks worn,

" Which, thriftlefs, fhe converted late to Shreds

" (Our Ridicule !) to deck their ftupid Heads.

" And though in later *Cloaks* fome· Grander
    Wights
                                    [Sights,
" Appear *(n)* Town-Whifflers to our diftant

                                " *Them*

(*l*) *Livery-Troop.*) The Attendants on the Honourable
High-Sheriff at the Affizes 1737 or 1738, wore *Blue Cockades*,
in profefs'd Token of that Gentleman's being of the *Blue
Party.* [*Many have followed the Example fince*, 1770.]

(*m*) *Vefture torn*, &c. On a certain former Election, a
particular very fat Madam (whofe Hufband broke foon after,
paying about 000 *Nichils* in the Pound) tore up her Blue Silk
Gown to make Cockades therewith, all the blue or purple
Ribbon in thefe Parts being already ufed, and infufficient.

(*n*) The City Waits, See before, Canto 3. Note,
feveral Don's of the Party have ---[i. e. *Had then*]--- lately,
by Agreement and in Concert, made themfelves blue Cloaks :
And three or four of them appearing in a Knot together
have been at a Diftance verily miftaken for *the Waits.*

" *Them* future Days with Black fo ftain'd fhall fee

" They'd, mournful, ferve in Death's dark
Pageantry.

" Strut they diftinct the while ;---till, fham'd,
they view

" Not *Blindmens Huts* alone affect their Hue,

" But (*o*) Coblers petty Shops, in mimic Pride,

" That mocks unwittingly, like vainly dy'd.

" But let not Talk from Action you withold:

" Prove right Your Selves, or than Yourfelves
more bold :
[Shout,

" Engrofs the Winds, and, with an Army's

" Blow hufh theVap'rings of the lawlefs Rout ;

" A Shout fo mortifying, it may quell

" Their Hope, fondWifh, and Longing to rebel.

" Strain hard your Frame, and with Elboic
Thruft,

" Bear down the faucy Headlongs to the Duft.

T 2   " Though

(*o*) *Cobler's*, &c.) A Cobler's Shop fituate near *St. Olave's*
Church. The Warden of that Parifh, in his over-boiling
Love to the Blue Party, painted the fame of a very deep
Blue, Windows, Stall, and all.

" Though—(as the Actor in the loyal Play
" Call'd CATO, in our Play-Houfe, us'd to fay)
" Though Mortals may not full Succefs infure,
" Let us deferve it, and do nobly more."

He ends. (*p*) CAMILLUS, for Triumphal
  Grace,

Like the Gods Statues with vermilion'd Face,
Did fcarce in Cheeks fuch bloody Luftre fhow,
As that wherewith his fiery Features glow.
He ends. The hardy Bands of *(q)* *Buff* atteft
Their Potence with prevailing Voice the beft,
Whofe ev'ry Throat with (*r*) JUNO's feems to vie
In STENTOR's Form, as pufh'd her ARGIVES fly;

           Or

(p) Camillus.] CAMILLUS, the Roman Dictator, in his
Triumph for taking the VEII, enter'd ROME in a Chariot
drawn by Four milk-white Horfes, with his Face colour'd
with Vermilion. But fuch Horfes fince the Expulfion of
the TARQUINS had not been allow'd but to JUPITER
and APOLLO: And the Statues of the Gods were wonted
to be painted with Vermilion.

 (q) Buff.] That formerly was the Term of Diftinction
affumed by the then low Party, *Sound* and *Buff* being the
difterent *Shiboleths* then, as *Blue* and *Yellow* now are.

 (r) Juno, &c.) Vid. HOM. Il. lib. 5.

Or (*s*) THUNDERSON's, reviv'd TERTULLUS, when

His Rattle feeks to lead our Leading Men.

More eager than the Sting of burning Thirft,

And rapid as ere *July* Thunders burft,

Right gallant as lift BRITAIN's nettled Sons

To fwinge th' infulting, proud, predacious DONS,

They penetrate th' inimic Prefs, and ply

Leaps, Reels, Stamps, Pufhes, to fupport the Day.

The Hall again takes through rubb'd Gateway in

Stir, Freak, Rant, Hurlyburly, ftunning Din,

That, as with colic Throes convuls'd, the Hall

Groans hideous, twing'd with the inteftine Bawl.

Scarce rack'd VESUVIUS quakes endanger'd fo,

When heard internal Storms of Fire to blow.

In

(*s*) *Thunderfon.*] If there be no noify, mobbifh, hot *Son of Thunder,* &c. who thus by the Nofe feeks to lead our Leaders, let him be fuppos'd only a Son of mere *Poetic Fancy.*

In gen'ral Tumult fumes the Conflict :--Wide,
Yet firmly denfe, the Swarms of either Side
With fierce Variety of Combat ftrive
Through either Hoft Difcomfiture to drive.

A Thoufand Feats, well worth an Ex'TER's
Praife,
[Lays :
And thrice three Thoufand Clamours claim our
But each Exploit would, but half told, prolong
In Folio Tomes,—defective yet,—the Song.
Wrath thro' the Whole in Conflagration fpreads,
And agonifing Spite Infection fheds ;
As mortal Bites of Dogs infane inftil
Like Fury, and a catching Luft to kill.
Each Individual chafes in Look to grow
A *Phalanx* fit to ftem th' unnumber'd Foe ;
As in each Arm, or Mouth, Decifion lay
Of Struggle fole to terminate the Fray ;
Or each impuls'd with more than *Roman* Zeal
Durft die (*t*) *devoted* for his Party's Weal,
And

(*t*) *Devoted.*] The old ROMANS entertain'd an enthufi-
aftic

And, bold as Curtius in his brave Career,
Leap'd in the Gulph, could plunge in Seas—
—— of *Beer.*

But doubtful ſtill to which the Day will fall:
No *(u)* Ballance Jove ſuſpends to weigh the
Bawl.
Nor Thee, Astræa ! with thy Scales of Gold,
Eyes, dim or jaundic'd, in the *Hall* behold.
Thy Bench in Heav'n by Faith they view, and
deem
                                [*Beam.*
The Scale of Haddy's Foes ſhall *(x) kick the*

                                 But

aſtic Notion that in Caſes of extreme Danger from their
Enemies in Battle, &c. &c. if a worthy Perſon among
them ſolemnly *devoted* himſelf to Perdition, and ruſh'd on
certain Death amid the Enemy, he thereby wrought Salvati-
on for his Countrymen, &c. Many madly thus deſtroy'd
themſelves.---The Earth opening once in the Forum, the
Augurs declar'd it could never be fill'd up till the Thing in
which conſiſted the Strength of the State was caſt into it,
whereupon M. Curtius, aſking whether it conſiſted in
any Thing more than Arms and Courage, arm'd himſelf
Cap-a-pee, and mounting a ſtately Horſe, *devoted* himſelf
accordingly, and rode directly into the Gulph.
   (*u*) *Ballance.*ȷ Vid. Hom. Il. lib. xxii. & Virg. Æn.
lib. xii.
   (*x*) *Kick the Beam.*] See Milt. Par. loſt, Book iv. ver.
100.

But what of that ? Too oft' we fighing know
Thy Scales *Above* affect not Scales *Below.*

¶ HOMER and MARO,–with their Gods of
   Old,
To ferve the Purpofes of Verfe, were bold ;
And THEM brought down, in Vehicles of Air,
With Mortals in ungodly Strife to fhare.
Good MILTON, haply, made a fpice too free
Both with the DEVIL and —— THE DEITY.
Monaftic Bards th' old Painim Gods forfake ;
But (*y*) GODS *as 'twere* of fainted Deadmen
   make.
Thefe Volunteers ere beats a Drum engage ⎫
'Gainft Infidels a Crufade War to wage, ⎬
And fight Heav'n's Battle with infernal Rage.⎭
To Purpofe more approv d might haply We
(If bent to tamper with *Machinery*)
                                   Convene

(*y*) *Gods as 'twere.*] To afcribe the Attributes of GOD
to a *Creature* feems really to *deify* that Creature. Such as in
any Place, and perhaps in a great many Places, pray to a
Man, though call'd a *Saint*, muft imagine him differently
prefent, and to *hear* Invokers in *many*, perhaps all, Places.

Convene a Chapter of thofe Saints who bear

O'er *Trades* and *Traders* tutelary Care,

Who, kenning thus our Garboils rage fo large,

Such Havock faft'ning on their divers Charge,

Might in the Clouds affemble, and their Heads

(Surrounding which a Blaze of *Glory* fpreads)

In Council join how War awhile might ceafe,

And made be Ten Months Interval of Peace.

(z) St. BLAISE, who — (if Monks neither
fib nor doat) —

Invok'd, whip! prefto! heals a (z) *fquinzy'd*
Throat,

Though with his Flefh in bleeding Tatters
rent,

Might come th' endanger'd *Combers* Prefident.

V   To

(z) St. *Blaife*, &c.] The *Legend* affures, that Perfons,
having a *fore Throat*, who pray to St BLAISE for Help,
are ftrangely cur'd.---*Wool-combers* look upon him as the Author and Inventor of their Art and Trade, and reprefent and
picture him as their Patron, with a Wool-comb in his Hand.
The Suppofal might poffibly be founded on his having (as
'tis pretended) his Flefh torn by fuch-like Inftrument as a
Comb.

To fave her *Coopers* from a mortal Quarrel
Might interpofe St. MARY of the (*b*) BARREL.
To juft St. JOSEPH ought our MUSE refer
The tugging *Joiner* and the *Carpenter.*
Bricklayers fhould St. GREGORY obtain ;
The Grace of St. ELOI fhou'd *Goldfmiths* gain.
St. ANN fhould *Grooms* affift, though none in-
voke ;
Ev'n *Butchers* claim St. MARY OF THE OAK ;
St. JAMES to *Hatters* might his Goodnefs grant.
Upholfters, fav'd from Fall, might praifeVENANT.
St. LE'NARD fhou'd no *Stone-cutter* forfake,
Nor MARY OF LORETTO thofe who *Bake.*
For *Taylors* the beheaded Saint had ftood
Who duck'd Repentants in Old JORDAN's Flood.
St. CRISPIN might his *Gentlecraft* relieve :
St. EUSTACE Aid to *Innholders* fhou'd give :
The Flea'd Apoftle with his Knife might fide⎤
The broil'd St. LAURENCE Safety to provide⎬
For *Curriers* and tough *Tanners* of the Hide ;⎦

                                                The

(*a*) *Barrel.*] Sta. Maria de *Copella : Copella* fignifying
in *Englifh A Barrel.*

The laſt-nam'd Saint might in like Wardſhip hug

Thoſe who *apply* or *vend* th' aperient *Drug:*

Nor leave of Aid the *Woollen drapers* bare,

Nor who at Wholeſale deal in Staple Ware.

The ſwarthy Artiſts ſweating at the *Forge*

Should draw, unaſking, to their Help St.
    GEORGE;

Carmen St. VINCENT have a Guardian Saint;

SAVIOR keep *Sadlers* ſafe; LUKE thoſe who
    paint.

Nay (*b*) JOB perhap for *ſome* had preſent been

Who've done lewd Worſhip to the (*c*) *Cyprean*
    Queen;

Since divers might, on *Scrutiny*, be found

With aking Bones who hoarſly ſnuffle *Sound!*

Theſe, and the reſt, whom canonizing ROME

Appoints o'er *Craftſmen* might in Viſion come

    V 2   To

(*b*) *Job.*] JOB has the Honour of being eſteem'd the Patron of ſuch as have the Venereal Malaoy.

(*c*) *Cyprean Queen.*] VENUS, lewdly worſhipp'd, in Old Time, in the Iſland of CYPRUS.

To Synod in the Sky;—and—(fince fo jar

Joiners with *Joiners, Smiths* on *Smiths* fo war,

Bakers at *Bakers* drive; *Wool-Combers* fpight

Their Fellows; *Coopers* one another fight;

That equal Perils from the mingled Rage

Abide the Objects of their Patronage)——

Refolve with one Accord to interpofe,

And by an *honeft Wile* difhoneft Difcord clofe :

That falutary Wile then in the Brain

Of fome fage FATHER, ftudious of the Main,

Suggefted might, through Vehicle of *White,*

(Invention's *Whet!*) or *Coffee* Steam alight.

Hence INDIGO, to counfel quick, nor flow

Of Refolution, nor in Action low,

Stout as TYDIDES, yet as NESTOR wife,

Might,—thus infpir'd,—in clofe Cabal arife,

And, confident of Trick-availing Skill,

His Fluency of Tongue thus fweetly trill :

" Copartners in the Caufe, whofe Blazonry

" The Heav'ns affect, as it adorns the Sky:

" Though

" Though would Occafion bid affert the *Fray,*

" And with *Mob Prowefs* vindicate the Day,

" Yet paft Events warn to beware the Courfe

" Of Butcher Fury and of Porter Force.

" The Foe *of late*—(Befhrew the Change !) —
have quell'd   [pell'd;

" Our hardeft Fifts, and Bang with Bruife re-

" And where a fmuggled Odds, by dark
Surprife,   [Prize,

" With Clubs in Ambufh, would redeem the

" *Law,* hamp'ring *Law,* — which oft' to
(d) SOUTHGATE leads,   [Heads.

" Provok'd fell vengeful on our Champions

" Remains it, then, that *Policy* take place,

" Such as may compenfate our laft Difgrace.

" For who forgets that yet o'er-clouding Shame

" Of our fo baulk'd, though well-laid, Stra-
tagem,   [Curtain drawn

" Which we defign'd - - - - -. (But be a

" On that Affair, a Night unknowing Dawn!)

                        " But

(d) Southgate.] The Prifon, or Goal, in its inferiour
Den, for Felons of all Degrees, and in its upper Rooms for
Debtors.

" But did,—opprobr'ous to our thwarted Aim,

" The happier (e) RECTUS to the Chair reclaim,

" The Seat wherein HE, twice fix Moons
before,

" Our Envy, and the Publick's Bleſſings, bore.

" HADDY,--you know, would his Ambition
treat

" In filling — as if juſt !— our Chieftan Seat.

" Be 't ours with *Guile* to diſappoint a View

" That with the Yellow would o'ertop the Blue.

" *Strength* were at beſt precarious ; nor we may

" *Now* hope *Adjournment* to atchieve Delay.

" 'Tis gone from JACINTH to prorogue the
Poll,

" Then in the Dark for Mercenaries prowl.

" And RECTUS, who as yet the Rudder guides,

" Though mild and courteous, ſtiff in *Juſtice*
prides :
" With

(e) *Rectus.*] Mr. SYMONDS, a Gentleman of the wor-
thieſt Charaſter, who was at this Time Mayor ; having
been elected the preceding Year (when he had been ſet up
only as a Stalkinghorſe, to facilitate the Choice of another,
though he had honourably diſcharg'd the Office but one
Year before.

" With Heart entire, and refolute in Right,

" No Wheadles lure him, no Pretences *bite*.

" As foon the PRUSSIAN, charm'd with FLEU-
RY's Aim,

[Claim,
" To BERGUES and JULIERS fhall renounce his

" And, drain'd of fierce Difguft, the PORTE
allow

" The envy'd RUSS to keep her OCZAKOW :

" As foon the DUTCH give felfifh Treaties o'er,

" And SPAIN *our* Shipping uncompell'd reftore ;

[Right,
" FRANCE toil officious in dup'd AUSTRIA's

" And SWEDEN aid, to get but Thank-ye by't.

" PULT'NY as foon fhall on Sir ROBRET fawn,

" And PATRICK's Dean turn Sneak for Sleeves
of Lawn,

" As warplefs RECTUS will afide be drawn.

" No :—other Management, prefage I, would

" Be his than that when manag'd JACINTH
rul'd.

" Wife Caution guide, then ; nor on windy Cry,

" Nor fpecious Colour, ever more rely.

" 'Tis

" 'Tis in our Hands, though *Scruples* might forbid,

" Our Caufe from Hazard of Relapfe to rid

" Were once more HADDY to fair Chance preferr'd,

" HADDY, the Idol of the hated Herd!

" My Heart forebodes, our *Fraud* and *Force* were vain ;

                       [again.

" Theirs were the Glory, ours the Shame

" But H E afide,—we may to Ufe apply

" Old *(f)* EXPLETIVE, — a Tool, for Years fet by ;

" But well referv'd for fuch convenient Hour,

" To chear our *Blue*,—and daunt the *Yellow* Pow'r.

" My Sentence is propos'd.   Advife, if ye

" Have apter Counfel, or with mine agree."

Thus clofing might he fit. And MAZARINE,

Slow rifing, might next in Oration fhine,

                        More

(f) Expletive.] Mr. CULME, who had been long thrown afide, and was at this critical Seafon pitch'd on but to ferve an End.

More fage in Youth than if ULYSSES' Pate

On green TELEMACHUS's Shoulders fate,

And thus addrefs'd :-- " Ye, Confcript Fathers,
   right

" On Me for fafe Direction fix your Sight,

" For a Dictator fram'd. And well ye know

" What Benefits to my Advice ye owe,

" Whofe Chin, fcarce confcious of the Razor's
   Edge,

" Yea ere its woolly Down began to fledge,

" For Years have, to your Wifdom's Praife,
   averr'd

" You mete not Sapience by Length of Beard.

" How large could I in pompous Strains declare

" The Greatnefs of my future Reigning Year.

" But Time fhall fpeak ;--And, in laconic Style,

" Be pleas'd to know :-- I recommend the *Wile :*

" Be EXPLETIVE your prefent Shift, fince vain

" This Seafon were my Enterprife to reign :

" Whereas Twelve Months improv'd aright
   may clear

" An Ope for fure Acceffion to the Chair."

        X   Thus

Thus might the venerable Daniel end,
And none reply, but, backing, to commend:
With Glee the *Junto* might adopt the Scheme,
And voted Thanks refound his Senfe fupreme:
Reduc'd to Practice the Defign take place,
And fit in Chamber with demure Grimace.

Such, fay we, *might*, if not aware that Skill
And Strength would fail a too advent'rous Will,
Nor *(g) Audience fit* unhop'd, we here affay.
But left we blunder in wild Paths aftray,
We'll ftill purfue the beft-known fafer Way.

¶ The Sun now, fhaping duly South his Tour,
Marks on true Dials *Low Life's (h)* Dining-Hour.

The

(g) Audience fit.] According to MILTON's very neceffary Petition to URANIA, " *Fit Audience find, though few.*"
(h) Low Life's Dining.] Twelve o'Clock, when the Vulgar or *fimple* Sort, fuch of them as have any Thing to eat,
particularly Journeymen Helliers, Mafons, Joiners, Smiths,
Taylors, &c. precifely go to Dinner: Of fome of whom it
has been obferv'd, or pretended to have been obferv'd, that
at the very firft Stroke of the Clock, they have left Strokes
of their own unfinifh'd. ☞ To prevent cavilling Criticks,
we muft here note, that tho' the *Freemen* are by us allow'd
to

The Thralls in SOUTHGATE have, with tir'd
    Ado,

Fifh'd up almoft Three-half-pence with the
    Shoe.

At WESTGATE Clowns lean awkward on their
    Rods,
                        [nods ;
And, gaping, wait 'till (*i*) MATTHEW MILLAR

Nor little ftrange at the myfterious Cafe,

A *Millar* fhould thus wear a *Collier's* Face.

Clocks blefs'd ! found Cupboard : Good-wives
    Belows ply :

Boys fpring from School, fharp-fet, with Exftacy.

Poft-Office Window, flap ! claps to : In vain

Pofters with Letters to fave Twopence ftrain :

        X 2   For

to be, all or moft, in and about the Guildhall on the Bufinefs of the Day, yet Numbers of Journeymen, &c. may
be, and indeed are, Strangers, and fuch as are not Free.
Befides, Noon indifferently, at any Time, is here intended
to be thus defcribed.

(*i*) *Matthew the Millar.*] One of the Images at the
Tower of St. *Mary Steps,* which, nodding its Head by
Clockwork, feems to affift in the Chimes, which play at 4,
8, and 12. They call him the Millar, tho' by his black
Complection --[*but fince the writing this Poem new p..intea*]--
he fhould feem to have been rather a Collier than a Millar.

For (*k*) STANNAWAY,--or Yokefellow in lieu,
More forward, fmiles the running Gain to view.
Now Trowels back unus'd the Mortar throw,
Half-driv'n remains the Nail with Half a Blow.
Smiths drop the mounted Sledge, and Crofs'd-
 Legs leap
           [yard ftep.
From Shopboard, and to Cooks or (*l*) Church-
The *Conclave* opes: Th' Affairs of Secret end;
Furr'd Gowns to grace the Nether Bench
 defcend:
But on the Stairs, until fome narrow Way
Opes for Accefs, prolong uneafy Stay.
As Armies, difciplin'd to Action, nerve
Their harras'd Ranks with Bodies of Referve,
Impetuous in, at once, Outftanders break,
WithVoice unbroke, obftrep'rous, to the Freak.

             To

(k) Stannaway.] Precifely at Twelve is fhut the Poft-
OfficeWooden Cafement; outfide waits Mr.STANNAWAY,
Poft to Honiton, or his Wife, to receive Letters (for each
of which he has 2d.) to be put into the Bag at *Honiton.*
[NOTE, *We fpeak of the Time when the Poem was written.*]

 (l) Churchyard, &c.] Here, they tell us, (I fuppofe jocu-
larly) Taylors fpend their Noon Hour, when they have no
Dinner fave Air.

To drill a Pafs now feems *Sampfonian* Toil,

Though *Staffs* of high Commiffion plowing
moil,

Thofe magic *Staffs* which hiden Treafure find,

And evil Spirits from Night-walking bind ;

The *Staffs* which dare thump ope robufteft
Door ;

Staffs which wrong-fided Drunkards fink before.

Work now Heads, Elbows, Knees, Heels,
Breafts, and Backs,

Till by detorting Jerks the Cieling cracks !

And, as ftretch'd Boots on forcive *(m) Trees*
extend

Dimenfion, Walls extruded feem to bend.

The graceful Portrait of the *(n)* Princely Dame,

Isca's fair Native, fhudders in the Frame.

Monk

(m) Trees.] Viz. Bootmakers *Trees*, fo called.

(n) Princely Dame.] In the Guildhall are at full Length
the Portraits of his prefent Majefty K. George II.--- of
the Princefs Henrietta Maria, Daughter of K.
Charles I. fhe being a Native of the City ; --- and of
Gen. Monk, Earl of *Albemarle*, a *Devonfhire* Man born.

Monk *eke* in Picture fhakes, as if the *Nofe*

Of (*o*) Noll with Vengance to his Seeming rofe.

Ev'n (*p*) Cæsar, whofe heroic Soul no Awe

E'er felt when He grim Danger inftant faw,

Cæsar, who on infanguin'd (*q*) Belgia's Plain,

And *his own* raging and *(r)* rebellious *Main,*

Shew'd Churchill's Self more how quick
    Fate to brave,

And Wager to fuftain the (*s*) wrackful Wave;

Cæsar, who dares, by Juftice led, defy ⎤

Leagued France and Spain, though flum- ⎬
    bers *neuter* by

The lull'd, feduc'd, ingrateful, (*t*) old Ally; ⎦

Britannia's Cæsar, with majeftic Fear,

In *painted Image*, feems the Shock to hear.

                                        The

(*o*) Noll.] Oliver Cromwell, wont to be call'd
old Noll, and his *Nofe* efteem'd notable.

(*p*) *Cæfar.*] The Picture of K. George II. juft above
already mentioned.

(*q*) Viz. When he was Prince of *Hanover*, and fought
in the Army commanded by the Duke of *Marlborough, &c.*

(*r*) His Britannick Majefty being afferted Sovereign of
the *Britifh Seas.*

· (*s*) Alluding to the dangerous Paffage from *Holland*, in
which his Majefty with Admiral Wager had like to have
been caft away.   (*t*) The *Dutch.*

The *(u) Lion*, trembling as if heard below

At once the *(x)* GLOBE's collected *(y)* *Cocks* to crow)

Threats to defert his Poft, and, with his Mate

Of *fingle Horn*, refign the Shield to Fate.

Bodies, on either Side, contiguous drove,

Incorporate ev'n to the Letter prove,

That from aloft Imagination dreads

Two *Human Hydras* with Two Thoufand Heads.

Ten cafhlefs Debtors in that dreary Cave

Yclep'd the *(z)* SHOE more free a Breathing have.

SCRUPLE

(u) Lion, &c.] The *Lion*, Supporter of the King's-Arms fix'd over the Mayor's Seat.

(x) Globe.] The GLOBE Tavern, where Cock-fighting is often held.---[i. e. *was often held at or about the Time of Writing this Poem.*]

(y) Cocks.] According to antiently receiv'd Notion, (but a Vulgar and exploded Error) living *Lions* ufed to tremble on hearing a *Cock* crow; as, on the other Hand, *Bulls* would fhed their Urine, for very Dread, on hearing a *Lion's* Roar; how truly let others fay.

(z) The Shoe.] So is call'd a little clofe Room in *Southgate* Prifon, where fuch poor infolvent Debtors as can't pay for Lodgings, are [i. e. *have been*] crowded, or crufh'd in together. It feems to have received its Denomination from the Privilege they, in Turn, have of begging Charity of Paffers by, they by a Cord letting down an Old *Shoe* to receive the fame.

(a) SCRUPLE the juft, who Raifin bites in twain,

That Scales do upright Juftice to a Grain,

Ne'er bought at WEYHILL, nor retail'd in Shop,

More flat, compact, in turgid Sack, the Hop;

Nor Smoke-cur'd Herrings he imbarrel'd chofe

For like Compreffion of their fquatted Roes.

Bellies protuberant and Shoulders crump

Expect to lofe their Prominence and Hump.

Heart, Lights, and Liver, fore Conftriction
moan;

[wels groan.

Punch'd Bofoms murmur, and fquelfh'd Bo-

Some *Galligafkins* to the helplefs Nofe

The mimick'd *(b) Gulon's* bruis'd Relief difclofe.

Damnonian

(b) *Scruple the Juft.*] A good old Juftice, renown'd for Strictnefs, and upright holding his Shop Scales, &c. &c.

(c) *Gulon.*] This being a moft voracious Beaft, when he has a Carcafs larger than would ferve for one Meal, he never ftirs from the Place till he has difpatch'd the whole, unlefs that, when he is full cramm'd, and can hold no more, he goes to find two Trees very clofe together, through the Interval whereof he drags and fqueezes his Body; and fo he gets rid of what he before devour'd, in order immediately to fall to again.

Danmonian Swains their grinded Apple prefs

To force Pomaceous Wine with Effort lefs

Than which the Stronger of the *Wedg'd* affay

For their PATRICIANS a progreffive Way;

Yet all the Void the gen'ral Squeeze may boaft

Proves but an Alley's Six-Inch Wedth at moft;

Whofe (c) tott'ring Sides, fway'd by th' elaftic
Load,

Next Moment clofe, and choak the petty Road;

Thro' which as, fideling, rubb'd, the Robes
recur,

To grating Buttons they tranflate the Fur.

The CONSCRIPT SIRES their arduous Tug
compleat,

And puffing gain their fafe and reftful Seat;

There to dilate anew the ftreighten'd Breaft,

And meditate a compenfating Feaft;

Y   Where

(c) *Tottering Sides.*] Meaning the Conftables and ftrong
Men who compofe the Sides of the little Lane thus fo
difficultly made; and fcarcely fave themfelves from being
over-powered.

Where, whilft go (*d*) *meliorated* Bumpers round,

The Hours. fhall. with. augmenting Glee be
crown'd,

Till (*e*) *Sir John Adee*, late, by Minftrel's
Tongue,
                                          [fung.

And (*f*) *Zwopping-Mallard* by their own, be

Severe *(g)* APOLLO on a Tide may laugh,

And JOVE on *Gala's* crank with Godlings quaff.

So (durft we, as your topping Poets dare,

A *low-life* Brute with lofty Man compare)

                                                    A

(*d*) *Meliorated.*] By this Word hangs a Tale of a facetious Alderman deceas'd, who order'd an Attendant to pour
out half a Glafs of Cyder, but withal bad him *meliorate* it,
pointing to a Decanter of *Port* Wine : And having taken it
off, turns to a Brother Alderman, yet' exifting, ---[*But
died long fince ; which I now write in Year* 1770.]--- in State
by him fmoaking his Pipe, faying, *Do you know what* me-
liorating *a Thing is*, Mr. Alderman ?---" Know what 'tis ?
replies the Sage, nodding his wife Head, " Yes, yes, I
know what 'tis : 'Tis *Port and Cyder.*

(*e*) *Sir John Adee*] See before pa.   Note ( ).

(*f*) 'Zwopping *Mallard.*] Another favourite old Chamber
Song, firft introduced and ufually fung by the grave Recorder himfelf.

(*g*) *Apollo,* &c.] Alluding to *Semel in anno ridet Apollo,*
&c.

(b) A tabby Tygrefs of familiar Race

Wiredraws her Loins thro' fome ftrict Cranny's
  Space,

In Dread off-ftript her furry Drefs to find,

And even Half her Intrails left behind:

But, after panting in enlarged Room,

Revives her Hope to meet a counter Doom;

Her fwelling Womb extends its flatten'd Frame,

Well-fcented Cates her eager Guft inflame:

Or, haply, fhe may with erected Ear

The Squeek of lufcious Game domeftic hear,

Nor doubt e'er long a Feaft of Ven'fon Cheer.

Augmented Outcries Strength of Whirlwinds
  blow,
                              [throw.
Threat'ning the heaving Roofs' puff'd Over-

Not when, on Birth-days, loyal Powder roars

In joyous Union through train'd Mufket-Bores

Of full Battalion, e'er a Burft fo loud

Was heard to fhatter an impending Cloud.

(b) Tabby Tygrefs, &c.] Meaning a Houfhold *Cat*,

The Welkin fkrinks, and ftarting Air around

Fears a Vulcanian Rupture of the Ground.

Command for *Silence* bids the Tempeft fwell;

The Word repeated does the Thing repel;

For *Silence! Silence!* with extended Pow'r,

From ev'ry Mouth refounding ftrive their Hour.

But Marfhals, who *(i) Stentorian* Clamour ftrain

To quafh the Storm, at laft, a Paufe obtain:

Then " O--o-o- Y-e-s !-- longly drawl'd,--as *Ufe* decrees,

" That Free Men (*of high, low, or, no Degrees*)

" To choofe a new Prime Magiftrate draw nigh'r,

" And Aliens, to avoid the Jail, retire."

The fage (*k*) PROPRÆTOR, tho' exerted ftrong,

Yet fmooth his Accent, to the buzzing Throng,

On

(*i*) *Stentorian Clamour.*] STENTOR, in the Grecian Army before Troy, is (at leaft poetically) recorded to have equali'd Fifty ordinary-Men in Loudnefs of Voice. Vid. HOM. Il. lib. v. ver. 784. Or the mere *Englifh* Reader may fee POPE's Tranfl. ver. 976, &c. or fee JUV. Sat. xiii.

(*k*) *Proprætor.*] The Recorder, Mr. Serj. B-lf---d.

On Tiptoes of Expectance, —All attent

Their Ears as THEBES e'er to (*l*) AMPHION lent,

To fuck the Charms of dulcet Eloquence,

Back'd with deep Knowledge and illumin'd
   Senfe, —

Yields thus his Oral Mufick :—"Gen-tle-men,

(*Their Style To-day* :--*To-morrow* Scrubs *agen*)--

" Since has the MAY'R his Confulate gone
   through ;
                                    [due !)
" (For which, moft worthily, our Thanks are

" I muft inform you,--(*though already known*)--

" It's the fix'd Conftitution of our Town,

" When

(*l*) *Amphion.*] The Fable of his miraculous Lyre, at his
playing on which the Stones which built the Walls of
THEBES, danced to the Places where they fhould be lay'd,
is reafonably fuppos'd to have had no other Bottom than that
when he invaded that Country, and carried Mufick, which
he had learn'd in LYDIA, then firft into GREECE with
him, the Melody was fo admired for its Excellence and
Novelty, that he eafily engaged the People to carry on the
Building whilft he diverted them with his Harp. Or it as
probably means, that whereas they were before naturally
rude and unciviliz'd, they were by his Eloquence induced to
inhabit within the fame, and live under Laws in Community
together.

" When call'd on to fupply the Chair Supreme,

" Your Governours have Right repos'd in
    Them,

" To fix, as proper Candidates, on *Two*;

" Of whom the *propereſt* remains to You :"

So, with a graceful Emphaſis of Tone,

TWO nominates, for their Suffrages ONE. ·

But fcarce the Cadence from his Lip can fly,

Ere Quarrel joins in one harmonious Cry,

Or but contends which Lungs furpaſſing Might

Could have atteſted in a lengthen'd Fight.

Difcord aton'd now in ſtrange Union ſtrives,

And Peace in unaccuſtom'd Concord thrives. --

With Culme! Culme! Culme! the alter'd
    Hall abounds;
                                        [ſounds.

Culme! unoppos'd from valid Throats re-

Windows and Walls feem Culme to ſhout:
    On high
                                        [reply.

Accordant Echoes Culme! Culme! Culme!

                                        No

No Deed, no Word, no Look, betrays a Fear;
No Foot recedes; all Hands Refiſtance dare:
All to the Palm diſputeleſs Title bring,
And, without Conqueſt, all Ovation ring.

Now lovely ſounds the conſentaneous Jar;
Now beautifully ſmiles, appeas'd, the War;
Now Party Battle proves a ſocial Play;
Now Wraths turn Friendſhip, bent the ſelf-ſame
　　Way.
So Winds whoſe Force, by Winds oppos'd,
　　might wage
A Storm, and laſh the Main to ſurly Rage;
But one Point blowing, though with ſtronger
　　Gales,
Delight the belly'd and more ſpeeded Sails.

Amazing Turn! -- Bells wak'd in Tranſport
　　feel
Strange *early* Pulls exhort each flinging Wheel,
　　　　　　　　　　　　　Whoſe

Whofe jocund Rounds the baffled Variance

    fun,

As thus the jokeful Confort feems to run : —

Victorious All !—yet none a Foe fubdues !

The Yellows loft not,—though have won the

    Blues !

End of Canto VI. and of the Poem.